slammed into inferno

NICOLE WATERHOUSE

CONTENTS

Chapter 1	1
Chapter 2	9
Chapter 3	19
Chapter 4	31
Chapter 5	45
Chapter 6	53
Chapter 7	67
Chapter 8	79
Chapter 9	91
Chapter 10	101
Chapter 11	109
Chapter 12	117
Chapter 13	127
Chapter 14	139
Chapter 15	147
Epilogue	157
Acknowledgments	161
About the Author	163

Copyright © 2022 Nicole Waterhouse

All rights reserved.

No part of this book may be reproduced in any form by any electronic or mechanical means, including information storage and retrieval systems, without written permission from the author, except for the use of brief quotations in a book review.

Development Editor: Book Bind Divers
Cover Designer & Formatter: Indie Sage
Proofreader: Celia Dobson

dedication

I dedicate this book to my husband.

You make me feel like this was something to pursue and never stopped believing in me.

Thank you for believing in me I could write this book.

Love you!

one

When I was a little girl, I had my life mapped out, however unfortunately life loves to throw a curve ball going a hundred miles an hour. So, here I am, a twenty-five-year-old, broken-hearted woman leaving everything I know and starting over by myself in Boston. Something which seems unthinkable, except here I am doing the implausible. It pains me because I will miss my parents, my brother, sister-in-law, niece, nephew, and sister. If I do not do this now, then I will certainly not do it later. I mean, what twenty-five-year-old is starting over? Well, two thumbs up for this gal right here.

I guess I should back up and explain how it started and why I am making the three-hour track to Boston at seven in the morning all because of by my boyfriend well now ex of six years. A few months ago, after getting off my last twelve-hour shift, of a three-day rotation, all I wanted to do was shower and have a movie night with Jake on the couch. I knew he had the day off and I was hoping we could have a night together as it has been a while. Pulling up to our apartment, I noticed my best friend's car, Brooke. Seeing her car when I get home is not out of the norm since the three of us are best friends. Walking in the door, tossing my bags on the entry bench while kicking off my shoes, I paused as I hear a noise coming from upstairs. Odd, as they are never upstairs together. The tiny hairs are standing up on the back of my neck wondering too why they are upstairs. I walked upstairs and I heard the noises grow louder as I get closer to our bedroom door. I swung open the door to see Jake on his knees on our bed thrusting into Brooke from behind. A position I suggested countless times we try. The tears flood my eyes and soak my face at the image before me. They did not even notice me staring as I am watching them go at it on our bed as I stand there frozen until they finish. Brooke screams and Jake jumps out of bed, a sea of curses coming out of his mouth. I finally came too, and I slapped him as hard as I could across his fucking face. I guessed my thickness was too much for him as compared to my ex-best friend, who is thinner than I am.

Not in the slightest did I have a suspicion the two of them were screwing behind my back. The only thing which makes any sense on how secretive who she was seeing, he was always busy when I asked to meet him. Well, now recently I know who she was seeing… my boyfriend. Assholes.

The fucking bastard turned it around on me saying if *'I loved him more and was more open to other things in the bedroom, he would not have gone elsewhere.'* Fuck you is what I say... they will get their karma for sure. During our relationship, that I had thought it was normal I had never truly gotten to experience having an orgasm, which was a struggle in our relationship for some time. Jake was the first person who I have ever been with sexually. I had nothing to compare it to, and I assumed this was what sex was supposed to be like. He was not a fan of foreplay even when I suggested it, but oh how he loved getting a blow job. Certainly nothing for me. He wanted to get straight to fucking to get himself off. Having tried to get myself off, I truly believed I was merely one of those women who simply does not know how to get off. So, I just simply stopped bringing it up and did what he liked. I was in love, or so I believed.

I truly thought Jake was the one. He was charming, funny and was goal driven. When we met in college, he chased me when I kept turning him down. Overtime he wore me down and I finally said yes, I would to go on a date with him over six years ago. After the date, we were inseparable and grew up together. However, over the years, the quality of being goal driven, which I found to be a turn on, slowly became what drove us apart. Work came first. Client dinner, client meetings, client events, etc. The list seemed to not never end, and it was always, — 'Evie, I need this meeting to take me to the next level. My goal is by twenty-five to be a senior partner. Don't you want me to succeed? This is for our future!'

I would cave for him every time, and I would stand in his corner showing my support. Sometimes I wanted him to put me first for once. Yeah, my job is demanding with its hours and can be mentally draining, however, it never mattered to him, apparently.

The last thing he said to me before I left was, "Evie, I need someone who is going to be there and not working twelve to sixteen-hour days. You are never here. I need you in more ways than one. You're selfish. Sorry, I cannot do this anymore."

Okay buddy, I was there for every cram session, each term paper, each midterm, final and while taking your board exams. Yes, being a pediatric nurse is demanding as is, especially being in a nurse shortage. My job has me working long hours, this is all I have ever wanted in a career, and Jake knew all of this when he met me. So, in a nutshell, these are the reasons I am making the trek down to Boston.

Saying goodbye to my family yesterday was hard because the five of us were extremely close. My older brother and father were about ready to beat Jake's ass when they found out. My brother was fucking pissed because of what Jake did. I mean, he and my father were not a fan. I however, chalked it up to being that 'no one is good enough for our baby sister/baby girl.' I came close to letting them both loose on him, but on the other hand, he is not even worth it.

The conversation I had with my mom made me rethink my mapped-out life. "Evie, sweetie, sometimes you must take the opportunity given to you and run with it. Everything happens for a reason and this, with Jake, was sad, but meant to happen. I know it may sound harsh, I honestly feel you and Jake breaking up and moving is a good thing." My mother rubbed my back as she spoke.

I am trying to wipe my tears. "Yes. I know Mom, it still hurts and fucking sucks. I feel it would have been better if it was a stranger rather than it being Brook. Jesus, I knew there was something off, as I assumed I was being paranoid. God! I truly believed he was going to propose!"

My mom cupped my face with both hands and said, "Well, my sweet baby girl, he was one of the many who will eat their words by letting you go. You will find the person who sets your soul on fire and will put you first, no matter what. Completely let your heart be open because it will happen when you least expect it."

"Sure, Mom." I say the words to appease her as I am not so sure I agree.

The cute apartment which I found a month ago while I was living at home before moving is everything I could have dreamt. Not sure how I got so lucky. Thank God for the sweet elderly woman who was searching for someone to sublet her apartment in Beacon Hill. I have discovered, it's incredibly difficult to come by, and I mean rare to find an apartment over here. Spacious two bedrooms, two bathrooms, open concept with granite countertops, white cabinetry and the most beautiful hardwood floors. The sunlight which flows in through the windows in the morning is stunning. I have the perfect view of the brick buildings and the cobblestone streets with the most gorgeous greenery around the buildings. This is what I picture of when I think of Boston. Even at nighttime with the old fashion streetlights makes me feel like I have stepped back in time. I must pinch myself to realize this is not a dream, and I am doing something for myself. Tomorrow is when I start my new job at Tufts Children's Hospital. Not sure how this dream of an apartment fell into my lap, but I am taking this as a sign I am exactly where I need to be.

Working as a pediatric nurse is not weak or as harsh as it sounds you must be strong to be in this profession. No one should ever have to witness a sick child hooked up to machines to help them live or even help their pain. I will go the extra mile to help them and their families by bringing some light into their day. Yes, I will dress up as a princess. If I must dress up as a superhero, got it. If I must learn those TikTok dances, count me in. Tufts Children's

Hospital is in its own different spectrum of hospitals for children than back home in Maine. Our children's hospital back home was impressive, although every now and again we would have to send patients down here to get treatments, which we could not offer. To be working here is a dream come true. Fuck you, Jake. I am doing it following my dreams!

I feel by taking this leap and moving, I am giving Jake two big middle fingers and telling him *'FUCK YOU'* I can do this. I do not need someone telling me what to do, what to wear, what to eat, etc. As he advances more in his career, he gave off the impression that my job was not as important as his. He was not supportive, nor was he compassionate anytime I would ask him to help with anything regarding the hospital. Nope, he wanted no part because it did not benefit him. God damn self-centered asshole.

two

The first month working at Tuft's has been going great and I am feeling even better about my decision to take this job. I have clicked with two of the other nurses in my unit, Sophia and Grace. Sophia is a firecracker and has a sailor's mouth for days. I have even learned unfamiliar words and phrases from her. I will say Sophia is gorgeous, with blonde hair and blue eyes. Grace is sweet and has the most beautiful red hair I have ever seen and the lightest green eyes. Grace is the opposite of Sophia, which works. We have only been working together for a month, and it positively feels like we have been friends for years.

"I am so excited for the three of us to have the weekend off. I mean, I have not seen this happen where all three of us off the same shift, but I am keeping my mouth shut for once. Leave it to fucking Karen to mess up during the schedule. Oh, well." Sophia swirls around to me and Grace.

"Sophia, her name is not Karen. It is Anna." Grace sighs to Sophia.

"Grace, she is a goddamn, Karen. Did you hear her at

the meeting yesterday? She was questioning her boss on fucking protocol! Jesus Christ! If I was her boss, I would punch her in the face!" Sophia mentions to Grace in a heated tone.

"Okay, Sophia, let's focus on what we are going to do tonight. And yes, Anna is a total Karen. She was questioning me on how I was giving the shift change their report. Umm, stay in your lane!" I agree with Sophia and her crazy terminology.

"See Grace, Evie even agrees. And fuck her comments. You give great detailed reports." Sophia beams at me, agreeing.... well, somewhat with her.

"Okay, moving on, I think we should check out the bar or pub. Whatever it is, I think it's on Boylston Street." Graces mentions by changing the topic so we can control Sophia.

"Oh yeah, I have been by there. It is ten minutes or so from my place. Want to get ready there and then take an Uber?" I suggest to the girls

"Hell yes." They both agreed at the same time.

I am feeling myself in my outfit tonight because I am not putting in the effort for someone else, only for myself. Sophia is a magical genius with makeup. God damn, is she gifted and if she stopped doing nursing, she would make a

killing doing this full time. She has me even checking myself out. Sophia whistles in my direction. I have on faux leather pants, which are like a second skin showing off my curves and my ass. I paired it with a black lace see thru top and a black bralette underneath which enhances my big breast. The bright pink pumps I got the other day really make this outfit come together. These shoes are not anything I would wear back home or even with Jake. Jake would complain about my clothing choices over the years about how unattractive I dress, and how I needed to 'put in the effort' with him.

He would say to me, "Evie couldn't you at least cover up a little? Everyone is gawking, and it's embarrassing." He used to like the way I dressed when we started dating six years ago. Tonight, is about feeling good about myself and spending time with the two girls who are becoming my best friends.

The bar, aka Lucky's Pub, is packed! I guess we chose the right bar tonight. It is what I imagine a pub being like in Boston: classic booths, dark wood walls, wooden stools by the bar; and the bar top with so many beers to choose from. When you walk in, you get hit in the face with the smell of hops and a mixture of sweat. We make our way to the bar to get some drinks. I am a lightweight and I know I need to stay away from the hard stuff. I enjoy an excellent beer. Back home in Maine, we have a ton of breweries. It seemed they were popping up everywhere.

"What are you bitches having? I am getting shitty tonight and then I am going to ride some D!" Sophia says ungodly loud.

"I am going to stick to beer as hard liquor and myself do not mix well. So, order me whatever beer you think." I squirm as I remember my sister-in-law's bachelorette party where I let Elise convince me that tequila was a great choice to have that night. The answer is no, no it is not. I thought I was seriously dying of alcohol poisoning, and I am a nurse.

"I will have a vodka cranberry," Grace says. We wait for our drinks at the bar.

As I stand up from the bar stool to adjust myself, I smack into what feels like a wall. I do not remember there being a wall right in front of the bar. Jesus, nice going Evie. As I take a moment to gather myself, I realize I slammed into a person and not a wall. I trail my eyes up to see who it is, and holy cannoli is this man gorgeous. Does this man have pythons for arms? His biceps are bulging from his big shirt and his arms are covered in tattoos down to his wrist, peaking out at his collar. I would guess his chest is covered in tattoos as well. My eyes travel to his chiseled jaw line with the perfect amount of stubble and those piercing blue eyes. Mentally I am wiping away the drool from my chin.

Then he opens his mouth with a deep Boston accent, sweet baby Jesus, "Woah there, are you okay? Seems we both were not watching where we were going. It is busy in here tonight." He says with a thick Boston accent.

"Umm... y-yea. Sorry...Oh gosh, did I get my drink on you?" I ask, mumbling to him.

"Oh, it's fine. It will dry. It is only beer. Did I get any on you?" he asks me with the ultimate panty dropper smile of his.

"Oh… no. Good thing we both wore black tonight, huh?" I chuckle to myself. Oh god why am I being so awkward about this? There is no helping me. Here is the most beautiful man that I have ever seen in my life, and I am making a complete fool out of myself.

"Let me buy you another drink, seeing as you spilled a good amount of yours." The Adonis of a man is staring at me, waiting for me to respond…. *Um, earth to brain, are you there? God, he must think I am a moron as I keep staring at him. Words. Evie. Words.*

"I appreciate the offer. Although I am not one to take drinks from strangers that I hardly know especially in a bar where I *slammed into*," I say with a smile. Oh god, he is smiling back. There is a dimple on his right cheek and he has straight, perfect white teeth. Am I dreaming?

"Noted and good as you should not. So, my name is Declan. What is yours? If we know each other's names, we won't be strangers." Declan chuckles.

"Touché. My name is Evangeline. Everyone calls me Evie, since we are not strangers," I say with a smile.

"Evie, nice to meet you. What can I get you to drink?" Declan asks me in a playful voice.

"Any beer is fine," Smiling, I tell him.

"Any beer?" he raises his brow before continuing, "Well then, let's see what we can do about getting you a fresh drink." After he gets me another beer, I assumed maybe he was going to leave and carry on with the friends he is with, but nope, he has stayed and is talking to me still. Focus Evie.

"You are not from here, are you?" he asks in his Boston accent.

"Well, you are observant. And no, I moved here a little over a month ago. From Maine, which is not too far from here." He smiles at me. Damn, he has a panty dropper smile if I have ever seen one.

"Evie, this place is busy, and I will get some D tonight!!" Sophia rushes over to me, a little too excited about the men in here tonight. Grace is following behind, shaking her head at Sophia.

"Soph, can you stop yelling about getting… you know what? I am not in search of some D," Grace says lowering her when she gets to saying 'D'.

"Good god woman, live it up!" Sophia sings songs. Now when she notices Declan is standing with me. I am surprised it took her this long to notice the Adonis next to me.

"Evie, who is this smoke show next to you? Are you

going to introduce us?" Sophia raises her eyebrows at Declan and glances over at me.

"I am so sorry about my friend. She is being, well herself. This is Sophia and this is Grace." I point to who is who.

"Nice to you meet you both. I was merely chatting with our *friend* Evie here as she *slammed into me* and spilled her drink on me. Being the nice Boston boy I am, I offered to buy her a fresh drink," Declan explains to my two wide-eyed friends. God damn his smile and dimple. Seriously, take me now against any wall. Oh my god, who am I?

"Well, that is Evie for you. She's a little clumsy from time to time. Happens at work a lot." Sophia chuckles loudly.

"The other day you crashed into Dr. Hallstead as you were clocking out," Grace chimes in. Thanks, Grace, for throwing me under the bus,—And I believed Grace was the sweet one?

"Jeez, thanks, guys. So glad you find my clumsiness funny," I deadpan. Jesus, how are his arms so damn big?

"I did not mind being *slammed into.*" Declan winks at me and I can feel my face heat up from blushing. Who am I right now?

I have to remove my eyes from staring at him. Fuck how are his eyes so damn blue? I mean honestly, how is it possible? How is it possible he is single? I mean, he is single, right? I think he is. There was no ring? Oh, my god, is he one of those men who goes to bars picking up women who are in a serious relationship? That doesn't necessarily mean he is hoping to get into your pants. I have noticed he keeps running his eyes over me and smiling. God damn his smile and right-sided dimple.

"So, the three of you work together? What do you do for work?" Declan is staring at me while asking all three of us the question.

"We work at Tufts Children's Hospital," Grace says as she glares at Sophia for chugging her drink.

"What do you do for work—Wait I'm sorry what is your name? Since our *Evie* did not say," Sophia says as she is wiping her mouth.

"The name is Declan, and I am a firefighter." Sophia's eyes go wide, and I can tell right now she is loving this moment. Grace mentions how she is going to the ladies' room and starts dragging Sophia with her. We all know Sophia is a moment away from saying whatever arises in her mind and it could either be a good thing or the worst. They leave me with the hot firefighter.

"Do you enjoy working at Tufts?" Declan asks me.

"Yeah, I do. The kids there are great, and it's comparable to the children's hospital I worked at back home. Do you like being a firefighter?" I ask him, as I have this feeling wash over me where I need to know more about this man.

"Yeah, it is all I ever wanted to be since I was a kid. My old man was one, my older brother is a police officer, and my sister married a firefighter. So, you could say it runs in the family." He chuckles, and his eyes have a sparkle in them when he talks about his job.

"HEY YO D! HURRY YOUR ASS UP WE ARE HEADING OUT!" We both turn our heads, and it appears D is him.

"YEAH, GO ON AHEAD I WILL BE RIGHT THERE TY!" Declan yells back to his friend. He then turns to me, "Evie, apparently my asshole friends are heading out. I am glad you *slammed into me* tonight and I got to meet you. Maybe we will *slam into* each other again soon." He says with his eyes running seductively down my body, biting his bottom lip.

We both get up and he stares into my eyes like he has done his whole life. He kisses my cheek and I get this tingling feeling coursing through my body. Am I really drunk after a few drinks?

Winking at me, "Have a good night, Evie."

"You, too." I blush. I am sure I won't see him again, bring this is Boston. There is about a million to in no way a chance. Throughout the rest of the night, I could not stop smiling after Declan left with his friends.

Two weeks later, I am sitting behind the nurse's station, simply charting away from the last patient I checked on. Okay, well, my favorite patient on the entire floor, who is the sweetest twelve-year-old boy. Like I have said, working in pediatrics is hard because no child should ever be this sick and well, Luca is vastly sick. He has leukemia, and this is round two for him. His parents said the first round when he was five was scary as it should have been, and the medication worked. Now, seven years later, it is back, and it came back even more aggressive. I am charting away and Sophia strolls back, bopping around the corner with the biggest smile I have ever seen on her.

I look up at her, "What has you smiling like a schoolgirl?"

"Oh, you did not hear?" Sophia is smiling like a kid on Christmas morning.

"Hear what?" asking her, worried because it could mean several things.

"Today, my friend, we are getting visitors from the hottest fire department on this side of the city. Engine

Fourteen, or as most women in Boston with a pulse, calls them, Smoke Eaters. I am telling you, Evie, these men are so fine it should be a crime. They do a calendar every year for fundraising for their firehouse, and *good god* it sells out in thirty seconds. I was lucky to snag one a few years back. Best investment," Sophia's eyes are wide as ever when she tells me the news.

"Okay, Soph." She glared at me for my reaction to her. I have no idea what is so great about this firehouse.

Ugh, why did I agree to work three twelve hours in a row? I need the money to pay for the amazing apartment I have as well as the city of Boston is not cheap. Also, I have the tendency to always say yes when a shift needs to be covered. Some call me a pushover, I call it wanting to be financially independent with the amount of money I will be making. It makes me think if I ever do take a traveling nursing job, I won't need to take overtime, I will make more for just signing with the company. The thought has crossed my mind a time or two as it is offered here. After I am done checking the supply closet, I notice the nurse's station has many women surrounding it.

"Umm what is this, Grace?" Confused to what has everyone in a tizzy. I mean is what Sophia told me true? If not, why everyone is acting crazy…. right?

"I am sure Sophia told you about Engine Fourteen. Well, they are due any moment. They are the engine that does a lot of volunteering monthly. They like coming here and talking with the kids. It brightens up the kids whole day and for once they can forget how sick they are." And now Grace is all big-eyed too over this? Oh Lord.

"Wow, this is pretty outstanding." Ding. Two elevators as pop open and out steps the Smoke Eaters as Soph said to me earlier. Doesn't everyone have work to do? Jeez, it is only a group of men doing some volunteering. Keep your panties on ladies. Out of the corner of my eye, I see Soph smiling. She must have spotted a firefighter she likes. Knowing her, they will be in her or his bed tonight. You get on with your bad self, Soph.

"Evie, I guess we have *slammed into* each other again." Hearing that deep Boston accent which has been haunting my dreams since we last met. I mean, how on earth can this man be so beautiful in jeans and in an Engine Fourteen hoodie with a backwards hat.

I turn and smile, "Declan, hey! So, you work on Engine Fourteen?"

He chuckles, "Yeah, I do. The boys and I are doing our monthly volunteering and we come here the most. The kids are so cool and if we can make their day a little brighter, then we have done our job right."

What he is saying hits me in the heart. Not only is this man beautiful as he is caring for others. Completely opposite of Jake in every single way. I would not catch Jake volunteering, let alone put someone else before him.

Someone clears their throat at the corner of the nurse's

station, "Yo, eyes off my girl!" I turn to see it is my favorite patient, Luca.

I laugh, "Luca, this is my friend Declan who is here volunteering today."

Luca narrows his eyes and crosses his arms, "All right. Friends are cool. Nothing else, man. Evie is my main girl, all right? I know I may be young, but the heart wants what the heart wants. So, watch yourself, brother."

Declan smiles at him. "I hear ya my man. You got great taste my man and I agree. Need to lock it down!"

Sighing, I stare at both. "Luca, we have talked about this."

"Girl, I can wait!" Luca winks at me as he says he will wait.

"Okay, prince charming, let's go see what is happening in the common room. And no clown mask today. My heart cannot take you jumping out of any spaces again today," I tell him guiding him down the hall.

"Ugh Evie, you take away all the fun," Luca wines.

"One, Luca, I need to change and flush your port for your next round of chemo tomorrow since you were being a big baby about it earlier and I need to get your new medicine to prep for tomorrow too. I had to bribe you with my mom's famous chocolate chip cookies. Two, clowns are so creepy and stop doing it. I almost had a heart attack earlier. And thirdly, I will not sneak in your favorite ice cream tonight before Debbie's shift. So, if I were you, I would get my butt in gear." Debbie is so judgmental and most of the kids cannot stand her because she does everything by the book, with no exceptions. These kids are sick enough. They should be having fun, seeing as they are stuck within these walls.

"Deal and one kiss on the cheek too," he says with a wink.

"We'll see. Now go before I tell Debbie you are the one who pulled the prank in Joey's room." I cross my arms at him.

"Blasphemy, Evie! You wound me. Fine, I will go. You promise me rocky road ice cream, if I was nice today." He grabs his chest, acting hurt. Okay buddy, keep up the act, although we both know I will get him the ice cream.

"Dude, you know rocky road is girl ice cream. I consider myself a chocolate fudge man." Declan speaks up and continues to say, "I know, it is so damn good I can see what the fuss is about it." Declan's fists bumps Luca.

Luca finally makes his way to the common room. Declan waits until he is out of earshot. "So, you're spoken for, huh?"

"Funny… uh, no. He is one of the sweetest kids, and it is a harmless crush, I'm sure," I whisper. Luca is only a kid, not even a teenager… yet, and his cancer has returned even more aggressive this round.

"I can see why the kid has a crush." His right dimple pops when he smiles. Damn dimple. I can feel my face turn beat red in front of this gorgeous man. And of course, the one day where I gave two shits in my appearance. This is what three, twelve- hour shifts in a row have me looking like; my hair is in a messy bun with strands falling out all around, no make-up, glasses, scrub pants with a long-sleeve gray shirt and my Tufts Children's fleece vest. Thank goodness he did not see me dressed up as Bat Girl yesterday for my sweet five-year-old girl who had her third surgery to remove her bone tumor on her right arm. Poor thing. Now, in hindsight maybe it would have been a better look than what I am rocking now.

Real looker over here. "I think you are running late to see the kids," I say to him.

"I do not mind at all. Maybe the universe is telling us something, seeing as we *slammed into* another again. You know, I have been kicking myself in the ass for not getting your number two weeks ago." Two weeks ago, I thought he was not into me. I guess I was wrong.

"Oh, you were huh?" Am I flirting? I think so. Let's see how horrible I do.

"Yeah, I was, now I am going to ask. Evie, may I have your number?" Blushing, again, I need to get a grip.

"Sure. Let me see your phone." He hands it over and I plug in my number and send myself a text, so I have his number. "I look forward to talking to you again Evie," he turns on his heels and heads to the common room. Okay, am I dreaming, or did I give Declan my number?

Slammed Into Inferno

Declan: Hey!

Me: Hey You!

Declan: How is my favorite nurse doing?

Me: Exhausted. I do not know why I do this to myself by working three twelve-hour shifts in a row!!

Declan: Shit! Evie, you will run yourself down if you keep doing those shifts. I once did two 24 hours shifts back-to-back. Never again.

Me: Okay, you win!

Declan: Okay, I am going to sound like a pansy, I am glad I *slammed* into you today.

Me: Me too. Crazy, huh?

Declan: What are you doing this Friday?

Me: Shockingly, I have the day off. Why?

Declan: I would like to take you out on a date, Evie.

Me: I would love to go on a date with you.

Declan: I can pick you up at seven? After work?

Me: Sounds good to me. Um, can I ask what we are doing?

Declan: Seeing what the great city of Boston can bestow.

Me: :) Cannot wait.

Declan: Me too. Goodnight Evie.

Oh, my goodness, how did this happen in fourteen hours? I mean, we ran into each other, traded numbers, and then he asked me out on a date. Jeez Louise! I do not think I have been this giddy in a long time and I was never like this with Jake. My phone rings in my hand, and I am thinking it is another text from Declan. Nope, it is my brother Eddie calling me.

"Hey bro!" Smiling at the phone talking to Eddie.

"Yo sis! How are you doing? How is Boston treating you?" Eddie asks.

"Um, it is going great. Shockingly enough, I have made two friends from my nursing unit. The apartment is a dream and I love where I am working. How are you? How is McKayla? And importantly, how are my babies?" I want to know everything as I miss them so much.

"I am doing good. McKayla is good, as you know, since you two text all the damn time. Your babies are not babies weirdo, they are eight and six. The two demons are good." He wines about my perfect angles.

"Do not call my sweet niece and nephew demons asshole," I chuckle at him.

"That they are, so yeah. Oh, I wanted to see if you have a few days off. I want to bring the kids down and obviously they want to see their Auntie Evie," he deadpans.

"Their favorite aunt! And you can let Elise know who their favorite aunt is. We all know who the favorite one in the family is so…. Let me know so I can see if I am working or if I need to switch," I tell him.

"I will tell her for sure. She is coming over later." He laughs so loud.

"Speaking of Elise, I need to call her. Her wedding is

coming up soon and Douche Canoe is in the wedding." Even the idea of him makes me sick.

"More like fucking twat. Oh, I did not tell you, I saw him the other day when I was on my lunch break. Little fuck saw me and ran the other way. Douche," My brother gets irate at the thought of Jake.

"Ha, he is a douche. Sometimes I feel I wasted too much time and energy with the relationship having blinders on and not seeing who he truly was," I tell Eddie softly. I mean, I let Jake walk all over me.

"You cannot dwell on the past, Evie. He turned out to be a douche who became self-absorbed and started pushing you to the back. No man should ever do what he did to who they claim to love, nor should they fuck their mutual best friend. The right guy is out there. I mean, sure, I will threaten whoever the fuck it is, Evie, you are a knockout. Fuck Captain Douche." My brother has a way with words regarding my ex. I swear Jake got lucky I did not let Eddie loose on him.

"Thanks, Eddie. Love you. Tell McKayla I will text her later and give my babies their love. Oh, tell Elise I am the favorite." I shout into the phone as I heard my sister walk into his house.

"Love you too, weirdo." Not even a five minutes later, my phone rings again. Elise. I am smiling as I hit answer.

She yells into the phone "BITCH I AM THE FAVORITE!"

"Um yeah okay E. Whatever your need to tell yourself." I am smiling so hard, and my face is hurting.

"Well, I do as it is true. What's up, slut face?" Elise says aggressively.

"Not much. Got home not too long ago from work. As I was explaining to Eddie how I need to call you." I yawn as I am exhausted.

"How are you liking it there?" Elise asks softly.

"It's great I am making some friends and well, umm…" I trail off.

"Umm, what Evie?" Elise asks me.

"Do not tell Eddie, Dad or Mom… I have a date Friday." I wince, telling Elise because I know she is going to freak.

"YOU HAVE A WHAT?" I hear Eddie asking her in the background.

"Damn it, do not tell him, as he will have a million questions. Yeah, I have a date and I am so nervous," I whine and scold myself for telling her now.

I hear her cover the phone and yelling to Eddie to mind his own business. "Shit, Evie. Well, when I am home, we will talk more since OUR BROTHER IS A CREEPER!"

"Yeah, he totally is. We will talk more about my date with a super-hot firefighter," I smile as I think about my date with Declan. I am already blushing.

"Sweet baby Jesus, you are kidding?" My sister is at a loss for words; no this is not happening, is it?

"Nope. Dead serious." Biting my lip to hold in my laughter.

"Yeah, I will need deets stat," she demands.

"Anyway, I wanted to talk to you about your wedding in a few months. I know Jake is in the wedding and you are not making me walk with him, are you? I know Luke and him are still friends," I tell Elise before she cuts me off.

"Listen Evie, I have told the piece of shit where he can go. Luke told him it was not cool and since you are his almost sister-in-law, he cannot support his actions. He is not in the wedding any longer is the short version of the story. I mean, he is still a guest. You are the Maid of Honor, and you are a smoke show and Jake was a dipshit! And who knows, if this firefighter lights you up, maybe he will make an appearance." She says it all a bit too enthusiastically for me at this moment.

"E, really? Can you tell Luke I love him even more? God, they have been friends for a long time. Family is forever. God, E! Do not jinx it!" I whine to her.

"You know I am, right? Yeah, I will tell him later. Shit, Eddie is yelling, I need to go. Something about I parked wrong. Love you!" she sings songs.

"Love you too." I miss them so much. I feel Boston is where I need to be.

four

The week dragged on, and it was finally Friday, and I was finally going to see Declan again. I cannot believe how nervous I was about this date; our first date. I face timed with my sister about what to wear because Declan was vague about what we were doing. All he mentioned was to he wanted to show me the real Boston. Elise helped me decide on my favorite skinny jeans as they hug my curvy figure and enhanced my ass nicely. I paired them with a white top along with my black jacket and finishing the look with my white converse. I figured we would be walking a lot and I do not want to be one of those girls in heels ending up with feet full of blisters.

Elise said I needed to add some accessories to keep it fun and light, so I picked out my gold hoops and my favorite bangles. Again, I did not want to seem like I was desperate, I am also a laid-back type of girl. I am not one to get dressed up all the time. If I could live in my sweats all day every day, I would be the happiest girl in the world. Seriously, I wear scrubs for a living! I called Sophia to ask her how I should do my make-up and well she said to do a smokey eye and a bold red lip, I was not feeling very *bold*. So, I decided less was more, plus he saw me a few days ago at work with my scrubs and messy hair bun. I applied some light foundation, a little blush, mascara, and lip gloss. Nice and simple. I chose to have my hair down, showcasing my thick curls. I will bring a hair tie though, in case I need it. Ugh, this is killing me, not knowing what we are doing.

While I finish getting ready, I take in my body in front of the mirror. I have been self-conscious of my body since I have a large behind, thick thighs which do touch and rolls on my stomach. Jake was extremely vocal about my weight over the years. His hurtful words still sting, and I keep thinking, what is the world does Declan see in me. Does he truly find me attractive? Having been with Jake for too long, I really started to believe him on how unattractive my body was.

Of course, right at seven on the dot, there was a knock at my door. I will admit I felt a little strange giving him my address, on the other hand I need to step out of my comfort zone here. I took five seconds to myself and looked in the mirror by the entryway to gather myself. Jeez, why am I so nervous? Oh, yeah, how could I forget I have a date with the Adonis of all men who walks into fires for a living? I go to open the door and there is Declan leaning against the door and oh, this man is everything and more. I need to squeeze my thighs together and push down a moan, so I do not make a fool of myself. God damn he is so sexy. Dressed in jeans which are so tight around his muscular legs. I mean, are those even legs or are they tree trunks? He also has on a black shirt with an olive-green jacket on. His hair is messy as if he just shook his hair, the rolled of out bed kind of a style. Man, he makes all clothes sexy. When he sees me, he smiles, and his delicious right dimple pops out.

"Hi," I say breathlessly

"Hi," Declan's voice is deep and raspy.

"Wow Evie, you look beautiful. Are you ready to head out?" Declan asks me while he trails his eyes up and down my body licking his lips.

"Yes. Let me grab my purse." Smiling at him. I need to control myself.

I grab my purse, and we head downstairs, once we get outside, I see he drove here. He drives a massive pickup truck. Of course, he does, because everything about this man screams, man!

"Not going to lie, I pictured you having a badass motorcycle and not a massive pickup truck," pointing at the truck as I was chuckling.

"Oh, I have one. Which is for another time." He winks at me, grabbing my hand, lacing his fingers with mine.

"So, are we driving to this top-secret date you have planned?" I am trying to fish information out of him about this date he has planned.

"Nope, this is a reason to make sure I walk you home. We are going to walk and take the subway see as we live in Boston and the parking is a total fucking bitch." Oh, my goodness am I getting incredibly turned on by his Boston accent? Lord help me.

We take the T to Little Italy on the North End. I love it over here on the North End because you feel you have stepped into Italy itself. There are clothes hanging up high from people's apartments, people are playing games in the streets, old men are bickering at each other, and it feels homey. We make it to Giacomo's for dinner. Oh, senses overload with how it smells like heaven. I love me some crabs and my body shows it too. I am curvy with big tits, with an ass for days, thick thighs which love each other with their closeness. My sister Elise tells me how much she wishes she had my tits or ass. Jake would throw jabs at me from time to time again on my body because in his mind, I was fat because I am on the thicker side, and he would tell me how I need to lose weight and work out more. He would complain my hips were too wide, my thighs were too thick, my belly was not flat, and it is hard to keep the girls in place sometimes, too.

"So, Declan no last name. Is this how you woo all of your dates by taking them to Little Italy?" I ask, smiling at him.

"Well, Evie no last name, this would be a first date for

me in a long time," smirking while he holds my gaze, asking me my last name.

"Cooperson. My last name is Cooperson," I tell Declan.

"Fitzgerald, Declan Fitzgerald. And now we have our last names out of the way. We are no longer strangers. Now, we are two people who are extremely attracted to each other on a date in Little Italy," Declan says, staring into my eyes from a crossed the table.

"Well, this is a great idea for a first date. It has been a while for me as well." I look away because I should not be talking about or even thinking about Jake. I have been trying to find who Evie is after ending it with Jake. For so long I believed my body was unattractive or how it was embarrassing for him. Now, I am starting to appreciate my body I have, and it seems as if Declan does too.

"You mentioned you moved down here to start over. Is it safe to assume it was because of your ex? I mean, I should thank him since now I get to spend time with you." He smiles at me. Jesus, his smile. I swear his smile alone could make my body combust.

"This is not first date talk... yes, you are correct. My ex and I were together just shy of about six years. Met in college, moved back home, help support him through law school, career growth and then I walk in on him having sex with our mutual friend. So, I packed up, moved down here to start over and put myself first for once." I fidget with my hands, and I slowly looked at him.

"Fucking asshole. He clearly was not man enough for you because you gave up a lot for him from what it sounds. He sounds to me like an insecure asshole who did not know what he had in front of him, which is a beautiful, sexy, smart, independent woman. I understand my ex cheated on me too, with whom I considered was a good friend." What woman in their right mind would cheat on this hunk of a man? A dummy is who.

Throughout dinner, the conversation flowed so easily, like we have known each other our whole lives. There is something about the way he is gazing at me. It makes me feel I am the sexist woman in the room. I certainly have not felt sexy before in my whole life and the hunger in his eyes has my whole body lightening up as if he has lit a match. He keeps touching my hand, my arm and my back, and over time, I get this electric feeling throughout my body with goosebumps. After dinner we stop and get dessert at Mike's Pastry. My pants are so tight, though I do not want to stop eating because this food is so good. We walk around Little Italy some more while he is holding my hand.

It feels good to have a man who wants to be near me and touch me. I wonder what those big callous hands would feel like on the rest of my body. We make our way to the pier to watch the boats and simply take in the skyline of Boston. This first date has been awfully romantic. Jake not once put any effort into any of our dates or were they even any dates since we were both two broke college kids when we met.

We both are silent as we are taking in the scenery. Declan is the first to speak. "Evie, I like you. When you slammed into me, you took my breath away the moment I looked into your eyes." I turn to look him in the eyes and my heart is beating so fast in my chest to the fact I am surprised he does not hear it. "And since then, Evie, you have been all I have thought about," he is staring at my lips as I lick them and back to my eyes while he is licking his lips. This is the moment he is going to kiss me, and I can feel it. And boy, do I want this beautiful man to kiss me with his soft lips that I can not stop staring at. He takes his hand up to the nape of my neck and leans forward and presses his lips to mine. His lips feel so soft, like pillows, and his tongue pushes against my lips as I open for him. I move my arms around his neck, pulling him closer. Of course, this man is a brilliant at kissing. The soft kiss is now turning into hunger as if we cannot get enough of one another. I moan into his mouth, and he responds with his own hungry growl. When we finally pull apart, we both are breathing heavily, our chests rising.

Declan takes his thumb and rubs it over my bottom lip. "I have been wanting to kiss you since I laid eyes on you in the pub. And if I do not stop, this first date will end with you in my bed. I am trying to be a gentleman." He smirks at me.

Blushing at his comment. I have only ever been with one man in my whole life. I gave Jake my virginity in college and the sex was well, okay? There is nothing to compare it to. I haven't experienced an orgasm. I mean no big moment, and I have tried on myself and absolutely nothing. I get a sense Declan will know how to please me in many, many ways.

"You are cute when you blush. I love making you blush Evie, your skin gets pink around your chest, your cheeks turn a like shade of pink, and then your eyes turn a little more copper," he is caressing my cheek as he tells me is a softer tone.

"Sorry, umm a little," I say being embarrassed.

"Don't be. I want you to be open to sharing what you are thinking or feeling when you are with me. I will never judge you." He tells me softly with his lips so close to mine.

"Thank you." I breathe.

"You're welcome." Declan says softly too, before he kisses me again.

Declan: I cannot stop thinking about you and our kiss the other night

Me: 😊 Yea. I cannot stop either.

Declan: What are you doing right now? 😉

Me: You know when you wink it's deadly to the women's population. Pretty sure it is lethal.

Declan: Oh, is it? I only care if affects you. Does me winking at you have the same effect?

Me: Speaking as a woman, yes. 🤔

Declan: So, if I were to wink at you right now, what would it do to you?

Me: Umm… 😊

Declan: Evie, I told you on how I want you to be honest with me. I won't judge you.

Umm, is he sexing with me after our date, not even twenty-four hours later? I can do this. Okay, Evie, do not make a fool out of yourself. Channel your inner Sophia.

Me: It would make me want to kiss you.

Declan: Oh yeah? Would it make you wet for me?

Me: Yes…

Declan: Are you wet right now, Evie? Tell me.

I am blushing because I have not done this with anyone or been so open. It should not embarrass me because this man makes my body come alive and I have only known him for a short time. I trail my hand down my stomach and reach under my undies and I slide one finder over my folds and yes; I am dripping wet. Holy shit! I have never felt myself, wet. The last time I tried to masturbate, it was a disaster. I could not get the motion right, I was not wet, like I am now. I tried to think of my favorite actor, Henry Cavill and nothing. I gave up and thought maybe I was doing it wrong or maybe everyone built it up too much.

Me: Umm…Yes?

Declan: Evie… Have you ever touched yourself?

Me: Uhm. I tried once and it was horrible. Shit, this is embarrassing.

Declan: Baby, that's okay. Will you touch yourself, Evie? I want you to imagine my hands on your sexy curves while I run my tongue along your nipples, baby...

Me: Yes...

Declan: I want you to play with your clit and then put two fingers in and if you can add a third for me, baby. I am so hard thinking about how wet you are.

I circle my swollen clit with my thumb and push my middle finger and forefinger into my sex. The feeling is so intense that I am shocked. I imagine Declan is playing with my clit while pushing his big fingers into my sex, then I think of his tongue sucking on my nipples, swirling around my nubs. Oh, my fuck, it feels so good. I pump myself with two fingers and think of how badly I wish he was here to do this. My whole body is tingling and my toes are curling as I am fingering myself. The pressure is building as I am moaning louder and louder and I can feel myself contract on my own fingers. It feels like something is building. Then it ripples through me as I orgasmed for the first time by myself, thinking about Declan. I chant his name as I cum hard all over my fingers. Fuck! I am breathing heavily, and my mouth is dry. I guess that is what an orgasm feels like.

Me: ...

Declan: Did you come for me, baby?

Me: 😊 Yes... I did. 🙈

Declan: You are so sexy when you blush. Do you feel good?

Me: Yes, I do. But uh...

Declan: What is it?

Me: Umm...I just had my first orgasm.... Never had one before.

Declan: 😊 Oh baby, we are only getting started.

Me: Oh?

Declan: Yes baby, next time it will be me who you come all over. 😊

Me: 😊 😳

Me: 😊 Good Night Declan.

Declan: Good Night Evie. 😳

I cannot get over what just occurred while texting Declan. How he made me simply cum as he was telling me what to do without even being here. Well, fuck. I can only imagine what it will feel like when he is here.

five

It has only been a few days since mine and Declan's first date and I cannot stop thinking about it or him or the earth-shattering kiss…. and well those texts. Not once in the whole time being with Jake did, he ever speak like that to me. I have tried many times to get myself off like I had the other night or at all before and with him saying how much he wanted me, how much he wanted to do to my body, I was a goner. All I needed to think about was his hands touching all my curves, feeling his soft lips kissing my body like he was starving, and staring into those blue ocean-like eyes. I cannot stop from daydreaming about it all and here I am at work thinking about this beautiful man. Thinking about it is making me wet…. god I need to have this man.

"Earth to Evie. Are you simply going to sit there and stare off into space or are you going to like work? And let me guess you are thinking of a certain sexy firefighter right now?" Sophia nudges me with her shoulder. I had to shake myself mentally and at least try to focus.

"Uh yeah, sorry. I did not sleep well last night, I guess.

And not enough coffee either. Yes, Miss Nosey Pants I am. He wants to take me to a Bruins game on Saturday. I am working until three this afternoon," I told Sophia and Grace about my date, and I left out the text messages out.

There are some things you want to keep to yourself, which ultimately is this. I know once she knows this information, she will be all over me like a horny teenager…. Hard pass.

"Ha yeah, okay. I mean, I would be too daydreaming of God of all men. Jesus, how on earth is he so sexy? I bet he is PACKING too! He is D-E-L-C-I-O-U-S with a capital D!" She laughs. I shake my head and agree with her.

Declan and I finally got our schedules lined up since our first date. It is a little difficult where both of us have crazy hours, so far, we have made it work and we have been texting each other none stop. Tonight, he mentioned he is taking me to a Bruins game. He was stunned when I told him on how I have never been to one before seeing that I am from 'New England'. The game was starting at seven thirty at the Garden and we both agreed to meet up around five in the evening so we could get something to eat before heading to the game.

I was excited to go to a live hockey game because back home, it was something we would do with my dad. We were little shits and yelling at the visiting team and cheering when a fight would break out. I certainly can be the loudest with the trash talk to the opposing team and I would sometimes embarrass my dad, it always made for a great story. I seriously hope tonight I can keep myself in check around Declan because the last thing I need him to see is me acting crazy on our second date. I mean it's hockey… he would get it, right?

"Number Thirty-Four, you call that a snapshot? My eight-year-old nephew can hit a better snapshot than you! Go back to the peewee team!" I yell to the opposing team.

Well, it did not take me long to show my crazy trash talking to the Rangers, the opposing team, and Declan. However, I imagined it would embarrass him by watching me screaming at the other team. Nope. He joined right in with me, harassing the other team and screaming at the refs. Man, Boston fans are no joke! They can be overly territorial regarding their players and, boy, they will let you know, oh they will tell you colorfully. As halftime rolls around, Declan asks if I would like another beer and I decline because I am a lightweight and I do not want to end not remembering this.

"Girl, you are something else, you know?" Declan asks me.

"What do you mean? Is it because I told the other team on how my eighty-seven-year-old grandma could move faster than their goalie with her walker? Shit, you would think they would keep their toddlers at home…" I deadpan to Declan.

A deep throat of laughter rises from his throat. "Yep! I have never met a female who likes to trash talk at a sporting event. I am blown away."

Turning and staring up at him, I blush. "I like hockey. Back home, it was our thing with my dad and siblings. It was what we did to the other team. I was the worst of the bunch because I would get right up to the glass and get into it. Sometimes I would bang on the glass too. God, my poor dad sometimes."

Outside after the game, Declan leans over and cups my face with his right hand and kisses me softly while caressing my cheek with his thumb. I melt right into his touch, and I get the buzzing feeling which has been happening anytime I am around him. The kiss turns deeper, and I could not give a fuck if we are in public in the parking lot at a Bruins game. Moaning into his kiss, pulling him closer as he moves from my lips trailing his lips to my neck licking and bitting. I want this man with every fiber in my body. Feeling his hot breath, he whispers in my ear, "Baby, I cannot stop thinking about you touching yourself the other night. This is what you do to me, baby. I want you to feel how hard you make me when I am around you and when I am near you Evie." RIP to my panties as he reminds me of the other night. Taking my hand guiding it down his firm torso, feeling the coldness of his belt buckle, he places my hand in front of his jeans. Sweet Caroline is this man thick and big. I give his hardened shaft a squeeze making Declan growl.

Right when I am about to unzip his pants, his phone is vibrating uncontrollably in his pocket. He ignores it until the fifth time it rings, letting out a sea of threatening curses, he answers. "This better be fucking important Ty," Declan answers with annoyance to Tyler. I try to pull away to give him privacy while he is talking to Tyler, Declan holds me close to him with a firm grip on my waist. Declan seems tense about to what Tyler is telling him over the phone. It must not be good.

Sighing heavily, Declan responds to Tyler, "Fuck. Fine, yeah, I will be right there. I am going to have Crowley's ass tomorrow. This is fucking bullshit and you know it, Ty," Declan tells Tyler in a growly tone ending the call.

Blowing out a deep breathe, Declan turns to me still with his arms around me tightly, "I am sorry baby, some dipshit at work decided today was the perfect time to pick a fight with third crew tonight. I hate to go and handle this situation. I am sorry Evie."

Trying to not over analyze what Declan has just said, however it is bringing back memories of Jake always putting his job first and me second. I understand Declan is the lieutenant of his house, as I am sure Tyler could have called someone else rather than Declan who is off.

Peering up at him, I smile and say, "Yeah, no problem. We will get together another night, I am sure."

"Yes, there will certainly be another night as tonight was rudely interrupted," Declan tells me in a raspy voice tilting my head up as he kisses me softly.

Is this what it feels like to be with someone who wants to touch you and be near you? If so, then I do not want it to stop. Will he be like Jake always putting his job before me? Can I go through this again?

The next week drags on and the weather is getting chillier in the city. Fall is here alright, and I am not sad about it since it is my favorite season, it just means my sister Elise's wedding is coming up soon. The bachelorette party is going to down here in Boston since, according to my sister, 'there is more action in the big city' which she is right. It was a little difficult to plan around everyone's schedules, mostly mine, since mine is a cluster fuck. The party is a little over two weeks away and two weeks after is the big day.

God, I cannot believe Elise is getting married, and we all believed she would be last or never get married. When she met Luke, the whole family knew how enamored she was with him, and we certainly did not witness her liking or committing to anyone before, since she would mention she was not interested in ever settling down. Since then, Luke has been part of our family and we could not be happier with them. I hope maybe someday I will get to experience what she has with Luke. I guess time will only tell.

During my lunch break, my sister calls me to talk about more wedding stuff. I love her dearly; it is the last thing I want to talk about right now. "Hey there, bride-to-be. What's up?" I ask her in a chipper tone, even though I am dead tired, as this has been one of the longest weeks at work.

"Sup homie! And do not worry, I am not calling to talk wedding crap. Honestly want to hear what's going on with my baby sister and this hot new man of hers…" I can tell she is grinning behind the phone.

I chuckle, "Oh yeah, I am good. Work has been crazy. I have been picking up some shifts here and there since I am taking time off for THE EVENT OF YOUR WEDDING! And yes, Declan is great. I mean, more than great Elise. He seriously is wooing me over. I said after the shit show of douche face Jake, I would not want to date for a long time, he came out of nowhere. Plus, he is so damn sexy." Blushing.

"Hell yeah, fuck Jake and his small dick man!" Elise chants, before continuing, "You know Evie. It was horrible how you found out. Thank god you did not marry him!

We all saw over the years of how he treated you like shit. I am now so happy you are happy. You just need to let everything happen organically. Umm yeah.... I want to meet this man," Elise says to me.

"Well, in time, big sis. In time. Right now, we are simply enjoying each other," I smile big.

She giggles before saying, "You want his big dick energy baby sis! I bet he is packing babes. GET IT! Live your best life. And hey who knows, he might be your person."

"Well, big sis of mine, we shall see. Alright, I am due back to work. Talk to you later. Love you and tell our niece and nephew their FAVORITE AUNT loves them the most." I chuckle and hang up before she can argue with me.

Maybe Elise is right on Declan, gosh, it has only been a few weeks with meeting him and the dates. She is right on the money, how much I want this man and the things I want him to do to my body.

Six

"Hey Sweetness, how have you been?" Luca strolls over to me at the nurse's station hanging on to his IV machine and pole. Luca has been looking a little paler over the last couple of weeks. This round of chemo has been taking a toll on him this time around. The dose he is on, doxorubicin is extremely strong, with the hopes of trying to beat his cancer this time around. However, being a pediatric nurse for the last few years, and seeing his most recent labs and scans, I am praying for a miracle. Luca is acting as if he is feeling fine, except it is a mask he is hiding behind.

I am working yet another overnight shift, simply the money on the overnight shifts is much more, and it is hard to say no. Plus, it is nice to take a break from the hectic schedule of the day shifts. I smile when he says it because the boy has been through so much and is only twelve years old.

"Hey Luca. What are you doing up so late?" I ask him because it was way past midnight and the floor was a ghost town.

"Gah I could not sleep Evie. The new kid next door to

my room is so loud when they are playing their video games. Plus, they snore so loud, too! It's like hello there are other kids here. Jeez." He is gesturing with his hands at his tells it so animatedly. I shake my head and smile at him, "Evie, I am a growing boy, well, a man who needs their beauty sleep. I need to be on my A- game with the ladies and you, of course." He winks.

"What ladies are you speaking of? I assumed I was the only one on your radar. I am hurt Luca," I say holding my chest frowning at him.

"Evie, baby, you are my number one and will be forever, I think this firefighter dude is some serious competition. I overheard Soph the other day telling G. So, ya know, I need to keep my reputation intact here." Luca tells me, bobbing his head like he is trying to believe himself.

This boy is one of the sweetest and one of the best patients I have ever had working at either hospital, it simply breaks my heart how aggressive his cancer is this time, and we are not sure it is beatable. I shudder when I think about it.

"All right lover boy, I can understand, but come to me so I can vet out these ladies you speak of. Nothing but the best, my man." I wink at him as I get up to get my secret stash of ice cream where I only keep hidden in the nurse's fridge.

"You got it Evie. Now, please tell me you have a rocky

road or this pretty face of mine will not look so pretty." I shake my head at him.

A few days later Declan and I planned another date and this time he wanted me to come over to his place to cook me dinner, which is one of the sexiest things a man can do for a woman. Jake not once cooked for me ever. Thinking back on our time together, I do not even think he knew what a pan was or how to turn on the stove. Did I accept his behavior and do everything for him? I guess so.

Declan texted me his address as I was going to be heading over after work. I worked a half shift today during the afternoon to help with coverage, as we are short-staffed with some people out on vacations. I told him I wanted to run home to change first rather than him picking me up. A girl needs to prepare for these types of things…. We need to wash head to toe, exfoliate, shave everywhere, moisturize our bodies, and then the hair, makeup and outfit. I am hoping tonight turns into more. It has been nothing but foreplay, and I am not sure how much more I can take before I explode. The messages are getting heavier and steamy and the phone calls, too. I am already clamping my thighs together and I am on the freaking subway home.

I took the fastest shower I have ever taken in the history of time because I wanted to take time to pick out my outfit and do my hair and makeup. I face timed Sophia and Grace on their opinions on what I should wear.

"I say slut it up GF. You want to ride his D into orgasm town all night! So, show up and bam! I mean, I do not see the reason to wait any longer." Sophia says eating chips and gauc on the phone.

"Jesus Soph! No, Evie, do not listen to the sex crazed manic on this phone. Be you. Be the girl he met at the bar and who he has been talking to. I mean, maybe wear some sexy undies and a matching bra underneath." Grace chimes in and zeroing her eyes on Soph.

"Yawn fest." Sophia fakes yawns.

"Thanks, loves. I think I have an idea. I bought that the new black bra and lace black thong the other day. I will wear those, and I am thinking my tall black boots with the heal, dark blue jeans and a simple a black shirt with my army green jacket. Thinking I will keep my hair down and curly. Simple and same with my make up too?" I am trying to seem chill about this date, I am a nervous wreck.

"Yeah, all sounds perfect...... Wait, you mean the boots that are suede or leather? I like either, the suede is more for a night out and the leather could go either way. You want to seem chill with a little sexy mixed in, not over kill." Grace says as I am holding up the phone searching for the boots.

"I say go with the leather ones. Save the suede ones for the bachelorette party in a few weeks. And diddo on what

Grace said....... Shit, I got gauc on my shirt," Sophia whines.

"Thanks bitches. I will let you know how it goes! Bye!" I sing song. Thank goodness for those two since I have moved here because I am not sure how I would get through this new stage in my life.

Right at seven on the dot, I am arriving at Declan's apartment in South Boston, and it screams Boston too. A two-story townhouse covered in brick with the brick steps leading up to the front door to his apartment. You can hear the neighborhood traffic in the distance. It fits him too because, as he has told me how his heart bleeds for Boston and it does for his whole family too. I knock on his door and when he opens it, he honestly looks so yummy and so relaxed. I stuck in a breath as I take him all in. He has on dark jeans which are snug on his tree trunk legs and sit low on his waist with an olive-green long sleeve Henley shirt which is overly tight on those python biceps. He has his sleeves pushed up, showing some of his tattoos. My eyes finally make their way to his handsome face and the right dimple gets me every time.

"Hey beautiful," He smiles and leans in for a soft kiss.

"Hi," I blush as he gestures for me to walk into his apartment.

As I walk in, I am taking in his space. He has it decorated manly, only it also gives off a homey feel to it. Typically, a man's apartment, I would think, they would cover the place in beer bottles and one chair in front of the TV. Nope, not here. He has some art on the walls, a nice couch set, some family photos around and, of course, pictures of him with the guys at the station. Maybe not completely a bachelor, only close.

"I hope you like homemade chicken parmesan with garlic bread. Because I have to admit I have been craving it lately and I might have bribed my mother for this recipe. And no asking what is in it," he tells me with a wink as he continues to stir the sauce.

"Smells like heaven if you ask me and I bet it tastes even better," I say as I walk up next to him at the stove and wrap my arms around his waist. He then turns to me and has me taste the sauce. As he puts the wooden spoon in my mouth, I keep my eyes on him and when the sauce hits my tongue, I let out a little moan. His eyes turned a deeper blue, laced with hunger. He licks his bottom lip with his gaze fixated on my lips.

He pulls the spoon away and I say, "Yep, taste like heaven."

Declan clears his throat and puts the finishing touches on dinner and plates it so we can start eating. It was one of the best chicken parmesan I have had in a long time, and I am stuffed. Throughout dinner, we chatted more about his family and mine. It's nice for someone to understand coming from a somewhat large family because it is chaos in the house twenty-four-seven.

After dinner, we moved to the couch with our beers to settle in to watch a movie on Netflix. I mean, I will take whatever I can to be closer to this man. The simplest slightest touches from him tonight and the kisses already have my body buzzing and I keep squeezing my thighs together. Breathing in his scent and being in his home is turning me on and I am doing all I can not to jump his bones. We are sitting on the couch cuddling and watching -*The Office*-, not really a movie, but how you can't not watch *The Office*? Declan has his arm around my shoulders, playing with my hair and twirling it along his fingers. He ever so slightly touches my skin and I instantly get goosebumps all over. He must know the effect he is having on me because out of the corner of my eye, I see him smirk. I have my head on his shoulder and I am grazing my hand on his stomach and each time I move my hand up and down, his ab muscles contract. I am not the only one being affected.

I can feel he is staring at me, and I glance up at him into his blue eyes, he then takes his other hand, pinches my chin with his thumb and index finger and lowers his head and I feel his hot breath against my lips. His lips then crash onto mine, and oh my god, can he kiss. His lips are moving against mine and his tongue is touching my lips, wanting access to my mouth as I open for him. I move myself so I am straddling him without breaking our kiss, with his hands are roaming all over my body, from my thick thighs, my back, my ass and my breast. I push myself into his touch more and grind my center on him.

Declan growls into my mouth as I pull his hair hard. He moves his hand up my shirt and pinches my nipple through my lacy bra, and I gasp. I pull back from the kiss and we both are panting. He arches his brow; I take my sweater off over my head and toss it on the floor. I try to cover myself up, he stops me.

"Never hide yourself from me Evie, I want to see all of you, baby. You are so fucking beautiful, Evie. I want to devour every inch of your body. Your curves drive me wild, and your body is every man's dream, baby. I cannot get my fill of you. I do not want to hear otherwise, everything about you is beautiful." He says in a raspy voice. Then he rips his shirt off, too.

Holy shit, I knew Declan had muscles as I Googled their calendar. Those photos do not do his body justice, I mean they appear more ripped and refined in person. I thank whoever gave this man this body because I want to trace every inch of this man with my tongue along every indent and crevice of this gorgeous man.

"Declan, please." I beg him, biting my bottom lip. "Please," I beg again.

"What do want, baby? I want you to tell me what you want." He smiles, running his nose up the side of my neck and biting my ear. I moan.

"I need to hear you say it, baby. You want my cock to

fill you inside? Want my tongue in your sweet, tight pussy? Want me to suck on nipples until you scream my name? You need to tell me. Because, Evie, I want to devour you and I want to memorize every inch of this sinful body," He licks my neck before he nips it. I gasp as he does it.

"I... I... Want... It... All..." I finally get the words out. My mouth is so dry.

He smiles and kisses me again; this kiss is not like the others. This kiss feels as though we cannot get enough of each other. He picks me up and my legs wrap around his waist, and I can feel how hard he is. He is carrying me up the stairs, taking two stairs at a time, we make it to what I believe is his bedroom, then he kicks it shut with his foot. I bounce a little when he puts me down on the bed. As he crawls up to me and places his forearms to the side of my head to cage me in and kisses me again. He moves his head down to my large breast and licks my nipple through my lace bra and I throw my head back because it feels so good. He bites down a little on my nub and I moan.

I sit up a little to unclasp my bra and I let the straps fall down my arms. He lets out a growl when he sees my full breasts. He moves to my other breast and swirls his tongue around my nipple before he bites it. I cry out with pleasure. He pops my nub out of his mouth while he moves his hand down to my jeans and to unbutton them. I help him as I shimmy out of them and then pull my thong down slowly.

He is peering down at me. "God damn, you are beautiful in my bed like this. I am a lucky son of a bitch. A man is starving for his desert baby. I want to feast on you. Spread those luscious thick thighs of yours." I do as he says.

He licks his way up my calf to my inner thigh where he bites a little and I throw my head back on the bed with a gasp. I in no way knew I was into being bitten during sex; Declan makes it so sexy. As he trails his mouth and tongue up to my sex, he stops and blows while he looks up at me with a smile. I see him lower his head as he licks my opening, and I cry out in pleasure. He flattens his tongue right on my clit. He is licking and sucking my clit with full force. I have my hands in his hair and I pull hard. He let out a deep growl. The vibration from him growling as he is eating me out has my body shaking.

"Yes. Declan… Oh god right there. Fuck." Moaning and holding his head right where I want him to be. I can feel him smile against my sex. He then pushes in two fingers into me and when he does, I arch my back and ride his face with his fingers in me.

"Fuck… Fuck... Declan… Yes… Oh my god… Baby… I'm going to cum." I am moaning and panting. I cannot hold it in any longer as the pressure builds in my belly and becomes too much as I cum chanting his name. He does not stop licking as I am thrashing around, clutching his sheets.

Once I can get my breathing to calm down, holy shit this is what an orgasm feels like. Fuck, this man is gifted. I am panting. Declan looks up at me with my wetness all over his face and wipes it with the back of his hand.

"Baby, you are more delicious than anything. I could eat this sweet pussy all damn day." In his raspy voice.

As Declan stands to remove his pants and boxers, his dick springs free, and I cannot look away because he is incredibly large and thick. I am licking my lips as I am imaging myself sucking his enormous cock, tracing the veins while swirling my tongue on his crown. Before I can act on it, he then climbs up to me. I place my hands on either side of his face and I reach up and kiss him. I can taste myself on him and it makes me want him even more.

He pulls back, smiling, "You like tasting yourself on me, baby? I want you to know how absolutely, sinfully delicious your pussy is."

The idea of his dick in my mouth makes me salivate, so I want to touch him and taste him. I have never been big on giving blow jobs, I simply have this urge to put him in my mouth, tasting him. Sitting on his lap while I am kissing my way down his jaw, down his neck, working my way down his masterpiece of a body. Licking every single indent of his abs and when I do, I can feel his muscles contract. When I get in front of his cock, I take a minute, as he is big and exceptionally thick. I wonder if he will fit in my mouth, I want him to go as deep as I can take him. I kiss the tip and lick his pre-cum on his crown. Then I slowly take in him my mouth. I get comfortable and swirl my tongue around and suck as I take him to the back of my throat. Taking my hand, I squeeze firmly on his balls, making moan loudly while he thrust into my mouth. I moan as I suck him deeper. He then pulls out of me, making a 'pop' sound. I am staring up at him, thinking I did something wrong....

"Baby, I need to be inside you before I explode. I cannot wait any longer," he pants. I nod to him as he reaches over to the nightstand for a condom.

I stop him, "Declan, I have an IUD. Plus, I have not been with anyone in a while..." I look him in the eyes. He arches his brow at me.

"Are you sure, because I can put one on_" I cut him off and pull his face down to me and crash my lips to his. Which is all the permission he needs because he thrusts into me and we both moan in unison. He moves, and it hurts at first because he is big, and I adjust to his size as he stretches me out. He hooks my leg to his side and fondles with my ass.

"Declan, yes, right there. Oh god yes." He moves his hips in the right direction and I am about to cum again.

He is peering down at me. "Evie, you feel so good. Your sweet pussy fits my gigantic, thick cock, baby. Doesn't it feel so good, baby? Damn, your pussy feels so good and so tight. Yes, baby, milk my cock." He slams his lips to mine, and he bites my lower lip with my moaning into his mouth.

"Harder, Declan. Fuck me harder." Saying that to him it is like unleashing the monster because he thrusts harder and my god it feels so good. "Yes… Yes…. Declan!" I'm chanting his name again as I cum. He thrusts one more time before he moans my name as he comes inside me. His forehead lowers to mine, and we lay there for a little catching our breath.

"Umm," I say panting and he cuts me off.

"Amazing. Yes, it was baby." Before he goes to the bathroom to clean up, he kisses me softly. After he walks back with a warm washcloth to clean me up, before crawling into bed with me, he wraps his arm around me, pulls my leg up over his hip with his hand resting on my hip.

Declan looks at me. "Baby, I am just getting started with you. I plan on having you all night screaming my name." I arch my back in response to his confession while he moves down my body again to my sex and I already know tomorrow I am going to be so sore from all the sex and I am not mad about it. Only makes me want this man more and

seven

After our last date, Declan and I have not been apart. It was like once we had sexed; it forged us together as if we could not be apart, which is so funny to me. Either he is staying at my place when he is not on shift, or I am staying at his. The sex is out of this world. I think we have had sex on every surface in his apartment, and mine. This man has a gift with his mouth, fingers and his beautiful dick. Certainly, did not imagine a dick like his, or any dick would make me so wet only thinking about it. I am addicted to his dick, and I have no problem admitting it.

Between spending my time with Declan, I have been trying my hardest to plan the bachelorette party for my sister, which is this weekend. I booked a hotel for the bridal party, planned out what bars to go to, pick where we will have dinner, and, of course, the decorations. The entire plan is to get Elise drunk off her ass and to make sure she has the time of her life. She is not only my sister, but my best friend too. Also, the good thing about her bridal party, it is only me, McKayla, and her two best friends Mia and Lydia. I also invited my two friends, Grace and Sophia. They know how to throw down too. Declan has thrown in his ideas on where to go during this bachelorette weekend since he is a Boston native.

"What time is this girls night starting this weekend?" Declan asks as we sit on my couch while he is watching the Patriots play. "You sure I cannot see you at all? I am off and I will get bored," he says as he is rubbing my legs.

"You're funny, and yes, no boys! The whole point of no boys is so we can get all the free drinks rather than pay for them. Jeez, this is bachelorette rule number one. All girls know this." I pause before saying, "These things get crazy! I should know, my sister-in-law was wild. And if you think you can ask how wild, I plead the fifth," I tell him as I am typing on my laptop, emailing the bridal party the itinerary.

"If I saw you in a bar, I would buy you all the free drinks I could because you would be the sexiest woman in the bar," he winks at me and takes my laptop and places it on the table. "I mean those eyes; those plump lips are screaming kiss me, and your body is what every man fantasizes about in their dreams, and I am absolutely a lucky son of bitch who gets to touch and lick anytime I want," he moves between my legs pulling them to his sides and kisses my neck.

I pull back to look in his blue eyes, "Well, we met in a bar and if I remember shortly after, you had to leave with your friends," I tease him.

"Yes, all is true, although I recall you spilling your drink on me and I bought you a new one. So, there is the free drink part. And I was a dumb ass for not getting your number then instead of a few weeks later," Declan says with his hands roaming over my body while kissing and nipping at my neck.

My body responds to his touch, and I am soaked. As Declan leans down and kisses me softly at first and nibbles my bottom lip, I moan as he knows what my body wants and how to make me wet. He slides his hand down my yoga pants and finds I am not wearing any underwear. He growls in appreciation as his fingers slide through my folds, and I moan and bite down on my lip.

Declan says in my ear, "That's right, baby, I want to watch you cum on my fingers. God damn, you are so sexy when you do. I want you to remember when you are at your sister's bachelorette who you belong to. Me. This body is mine. This pussy is mine. I need to hear you say it, baby." He rubs my clit with his thumb while takes he index and middle finger sliding them deep inside me. Making me cry out with pleasure.

I ride his fingers eagerly. "Oh Declan, y-y-yes right there, baby. Jesus fuck!" I gasp at him.

He stops and I let out a whimper. "You did not answer me. I will not let you cum until I hear you tell me." Those piercing blue eyes are staring right through me.

"Yours," I whisper.

He smiles, "Good girl."

He moves his fingers and then curves them to left and I lose it. I cum so hard on his fingers with my whole body shaking from the intensity of the orgasm.

He drags his fingers out and sticks his two fingers in his mouth. "My favorite flavor." He goes back to rubbing my legs, it is all I can think about is tasting him and I want his dick in my mouth so badly.

I pull his hands away and get up in front of him. I push him back on the couch and kneel in front of him. He arches his eyebrow at me and says, "Evie, do not feel you have to suck my cock because I fingered you, baby. I love watching your cum as you are so beautiful when you do."

I smile at him, "Dec, I want to." I reach to pull his gray sweatpants down and he has no boxers on. He is still hard from getting me off with his fingers. I lick my lips and lower myself to his crown, while I lick the pre-cum off him and slowly take him in the mouth. He tastes like salt and his scent. He throws his head back and his right hand is cupping my face.

"Jesus Evie, yes, exactly like---baby. Fuck!" I swirl my tongue around his shaft, and I cup his balls and squeeze them a little.

"Evie! Fuck... y-y-yes, baby. I want to cum in your sexy mouth." As he is close, I can feel his shaft throbbing. Wanting to take him deeper in my mouth, I gag a little. Breathing through my nose, relaxing my throat, I start to move up and down his length while cupping his balls in my left hand. Taking him all the to the back of my throat, "Evie, baby, I am going to…" He did not even get to finish as his cum shot down my throat and he grabs my hair as he finishes.

When he is done, I pop him out and wipe the corners of my mouth. He pulls me up to kiss me hard. "Baby, that was amazing. Your mouth is sinful." I smile at him and kiss him once more. We go back to doing what we were doing before our playtime.

The bachelorette party is finally here, and I am so excited for my sister. She and her friends got a room at The Copley Plaza for a great price. I checked in before everyone arrived, although I was not staying tonight. I prefer my bed rather than sharing it with six drunk girls. Grace and Sophia are not staying either. I decorated the entire room with cutout penises of Luke and unpacked the snacks and drinks. Elise is going to be so excited!

"Evie, this is amazing! You seriously outdid yourself here and I truly have the best sister/best friend in the world! GAH I AM GETTING MARRIED!!" Elise shouts in excitement.

"Yes, you are my sister! And you deserve the best!" I hug her. "All right, well, here is what we are doing tonight.

First, we will get ready here. Get all sexed up, dinner at a nice restaurant, then we are hitting the town tonight lady! Get ready to be fucked up on your last night of single womanhood," I tell my sister.

"Here's to ELISE! TO THE SAME PENIS FOREVER!" I chant and we all take a shot.

We all get ready in the room. The instructions I gave my sister, and to the girls, was she was to wear white. Either a dress, romper, whatever she wanted, and then us girls were to wear black in some form. I am not sure what it is since being with Declan, I am feeling myself; I am more confident in my body, and I am not ashamed if I wear something which might be too tight or too revealing. He tells me countlessly how much he loves my body.

The dress I am wearing is out of my comfort zone, I feel good about it. I found this corset dress from Shien online. The material is so soft and stretchy which I do not find a lot in women's clothing. It has thin straps, and the bodice is super tight, which pushes the girls together. I have big tits and this dress makes them seem even bigger. The lower half is a little looser, still tight around the hips and ass. The dress is short. Shorter than I am used to wearing and I am paring it with my thigh high black suede boots. They give me an extra few inches as I am 5'5. I choose to leave my hair down curly, and Sophia is a magician with make-up. I told her I wanted sexy, yet natural. A light smoky eye with false lashes, a little highlight on the apple of my cheeks and, to finish it, a bold red lip. I usually stay away from a color on my lips, though seeing myself all done up, I am even at a loss for words.

I am still gawking at myself, and Elise walks up to me, "Look at my baby sister who is a god damn smoke show. Damn girlfriend, where have you been hiding? I bet Declan cannot keep his hands to himself."

I smile at her in the mirror and say, "Thanks, sister. You are correct on the last part." I blush at her. I turn around and face her, "Love you and I want you to have the best night ever. You deserve it."

"Evie, you have done more than enough. Now, let's take a sexy picture of you and send to it your sex on a stick of a boyfriend. And you are bringing him to the wedding. There is no 'Ifs or And's about it." I turn and pose for the picture. Before sending to Declan, I am studying the picture because I do not think in the past six years, I have ever felt this sexy.

Me: '**IMAGE**' Already to hit the town. What do you think 😏

Declan: JESUS FUCK EVIE! Fuck, you sure know how to give a man a freaking heart attack and boner all in one. You sure you have to go? You could come over here and ride my face all night 😈 🍆 💦

Me: As much as I want to do all those things, babe, I have to go out. I need to get the bride free drinks tonight 😊

Declan: 😐 Behave.

Me: I always behave baby 😇

Declan: 😊 Be safe baby. And remember… you're MINE.

We finished dinner and made it to the club highly suggested to me by Declan. It is what you would imagine a dance club to be like, with laser-colored lights and a DJ at the back of the club. Elise has on her sash with *'I'm The Bride'* written on it, along with a tiara and a veil.

Walking up to the bar waiting to order our first round of drinks, there is a group of guys getting theirs. They noticed us and bought us all a round of shots. I was already tipsy from the drinks at dinner and then this shot. I do not want to be too drunk and not remember anything, so I have switched to water. The girls take their drinks, and we move to the dance floor.

Sophia is in her element because, for whatever reason, the men here tonight are so hot. She is drooling at the sight of all the men. "It's like I am in a candy store, and I want to taste all the flavors. COME TO MAMA!!" Sophia strides over to a group of men over near us and she is going to make her shot.

Let's be real here. She will go home with one of them tonight. Elise, Lydia, Mia and McKayla are dancing, having the time of their lives and the drinks are flowing for those ladies. McKayla needs a mom's night out and Elise is letting loose before she ties the knot. Hard to believe how I assumed Jake was going to propose all those months ago and now I am so happy he did not. Not happy how I found out, I would not be living here, making new friends, and of course I would certainly not have met Declan.

I am dancing and enjoying this time with my sister and friends, and I feel someone approach me. I stiffen up because I am not one who dances with random guys at clubs. His arm wraps around me and I would recognize his scent of musk and spice and those tattoos on his arms. It is Declan.

I push into him, and he runs his nose against my neck and say, "I could not stay away from you tonight and the picture you sent me earlier is much sexier in person. Plus, I couldn't stand all these other mother fuckers thinking they can have what is mine. I need you, baby. I want to pin you against the wall and stick my enormous cock into your tight pussy, which drives me insane."

I grind my ass into his groin while we dance. He is grabbing my hips, and he growls in my ear. I am beyond wet at this point. This man can make me wet simply by the thought of him because he has some possession over my body, and I am okay with how he is possessive of my body.

He leans in and says to me, "Baby, if you keep it up, I will not be gentle because I will fuck your tight pussy hard, and you will be sore tomorrow."

I turn to his front and mouth, "Prove it." I bat my eyes at him.

"Baby, I have already jerked off twice to your photo and I cannot wait anymore to sink into your tight pussy with you screaming my name. You in this dress and boots is downright sinful. It will be fast baby, because I am not going to last long." He growls as he moves closer to me.

The next thing I know he is dragging me through the club towards the restrooms. The women's room already has a line and the men's does too. We walk to the other end of the hallway, where it is darker than the front. There is a door and Declan tries the door handle, and it opens. It is a storage locker which works for me. He shuts the door with force and locks the door and then pins me against it. I am already panting, and we have not even kissed yet. I need to have him in me now before I lose my ever-loving mind.

The darkness is all around us and the only sounds are from our heavy breathing as Declan grabs the nap of my neck to pull me closer slamming his lips on to mine. The kiss is not gentle at all as he is kissing with pure hunger behind it. Grabbing my ass hard, knowing there will be a handprint after. I go to wrap my legs around his middle, and I feel his erection on my stomach. God, I want to him in me now. I hear him unfasten his belt and then unzip his pants. Just the anticipation is making me soaking wet. He trails his fingers tips down my body and when he reaches my sex; he rips the tiny fabric from my body and shoves it in his pocket. Declan then slams into me without warning unleashing a deep growl. I moan loudly and as he is thrusting in and out of me hard. God, he feels so good.

He trails his hand to my ass and slaps it. I moan even louder. "You like it when I spank you, baby? I love this ass and someday I will own this ass like I own your pussy. Next time, I will spank you until you cum," Declan whispers in my ear. He spins us around, so my front is against the wall of the storage room. The image he painted of him fucking my ass makes me even wetter while he is fucking me in this storage closet.

"D-D-Declan! Yes, right there… F… Fuc… Fu…. Fuck… Yes… Harder Declan… Shit!" I shout at him.

Thankfully, no one can hear us over the music. He moves his left hand to the front of us and starts rubbing my clit while he thrusts into me harder into the wall where there is going to be a bruise. I feel the tightness in my stomach, and I am so close. I can feel he is close too as his shaft is pulsing inside me… Declan thrusts into me harder, and I feel his dick pulsate and he cums inside me, "Fuck, Evie…."

Declan slides out of me slowly turning, resting his

head on my shoulder, while we both are panting with himself still inside me and says, "Please stay with me tonight?"

I smile and pull back to get a good look at him and say, "Yes I can." He drags out of me and helps adjust my dress and I help adjust him too. We make our way back to the club, holding each other close. How am I already falling for this man, and it has only been two months?

eight

Elise's wedding day had finally made it and I could not be any more excited to share this special day with her by her side. However, I am nervous this is the first time Declan will meet my family besides Elise. When she met him at her bachelorette party, her eyes about jumped out of their sockets.

The wedding is being held at 'The Red Barn' in South Berwick, Maine, which is located outside of York. When Elise showed me this venue, my mouth dropped at how breathtaking the location was and what she was envisioning for her big day. The barn itself has high wooden beams traveling up to the ceiling and the chandlers give the room a romantic feel, transporting you to somewhere else. She could not have picked a better venue for the wedding of her dreams.

The bridesmaid dresses Elise had chosen are gorgeous sage green chiffon dresses with ruffle cap sleeves. The top is a sweetheart neckline, a tight bodice, and it flows out to a-line cut with a slit up the right side. She had us in nude heels of our choosing. The dress flows and fits all our different body types. When she showed me the dress months ago, at first, I was concerned about how it would look on everyone since we are all different body shapes, especially, myself on the thicker side. However, it fits everyone beautifully.

Elise's wedding dress is a mermaid fit, and the bodice is super tight and with a sweetheart neckline ruffle cape sleeves to match our dresses. The dress has lace all over with cutouts under the bust line with the back all open to her lower back. The bottom half flows out with lace and tulle. Her train is long with the same detail as the dress. She chose to not go with a veil opting a few flowers in her hair. Her hair is down and curled with one side pinned behind her ear, pairing it with a white orchid. My eyes water staring at my big sister on how breath taking she looks, no tears as I will need to have my makeup redone before the wedding even starts. The wedding is taking place inside since it is a late fall in Maine, and we are near the ocean. If it was outside, I would freeze my tits off. Maine's weather can be a touchy sometimes, as weather can change on a dime in seconds.

We are all lined up and ready to walk down the aisle and I turn to watch my sister and our dad have their moment. I am trying to fight back my tears because it is such a touching moment to watch because our family is so close. It makes me think of my special day and when my dad gets to walk me down the aisle. As I am thinking about my day, I turn and get a sneak peek of the guests and I catch Declan talking with some of my family. I smile and think maybe this man I have been dating for two months could be the one I walk down the aisle to. I cannot get caught in a dream or whatever you would call it because I honestly do not think it is in the cards for me. Jake did a number on myself-worth, and it is still a work in progress.

The music starts and McKayla makes her way down the aisle, and I have to say my sister-law is drop dead gorgeous and I do not have the slightest idea on how in the hell my brother pulled her. I mean, yeah; he is attractive, he is also a complete nerd. My brother steps out into the lineup of groomsmen to give her a kiss. Okay, okay, he got some major brownie points. Mia makes her way down the aisle, and next is Lydia.

Then there is me and before I head down the aisle, I look back at my sister and joke with her, "There is still time. I can run and get the car and we can blow this popsicle stand, sis. Say the word." She simply laughs at me.

I turn and walk down the aisle. I lock eyes with Declan, whose eyes sparkle at me as I am walking down. He winks at me when I get close and it's all I can do to not have my legs give out on me. Nolan and Rose, our niece and nephew, walk after me ahead of my sister. They look adorable in the matching outfits to the bridal party. It is as if my ovaries are in screaming *'make babies right now'* and no cool your jets. Nolan walks up to Luke and does the finger eye point as he is watching him. It is a joke because those two kids love Luke and Luke loves them.

The music changes and my dad and sister are walking down the aisle and there is pure joy on my dad's face as he is walking down to give Elsie away. Our dad is the biggest softie, and his two little girls are the apples of his eye. I can tell how hard it is for him to let go one of his baby girls go.

Then I turn to look at Luke, who is bawling like a big baby watching the love of his life walk toward him. My sister looks like an absolute angel, and you can feel the love they both share with each other because my sister is crying, and she has a vice grip on my poor dad's hand. My dad is crying too. Once Elise gets to the altar, I take her bouquet and fix her dress. During their vows I turn, and I lock eyes again with Declan and my whole body is buzzing. We are staring at each other during the whole ceremony, and it is only when everyone cheers; I break the current between us. As I am walking out with the best man, I glance over to see Jake is sitting with Brooke. No surprise there, as I have heard they are dating; good, she can have him.

The reception is underway, and we have done all the typical things one does at a wedding: cutting the cake, first dance, garter toss, bouquet toss, and speeches. Glad this is all over and I can spend time on my date. Finally, being able to catch my breath after all the *'maid of honor'* duties are all said and done, I make my way over to the bar to get myself a much-needed beer. As I am waiting for my drink, I see someone approach out the corner of my eye step up to the bar next to me, Jake. Fuck my life.

"Surprised you found someone who is attracted to you Evie, seeing as you never have any time to date anyone. How long has this been going on? Were you already fucking him while we were together?" I could feel his voice dripping in anger and hatred towards me. I would usually let this affect me, nope not this time. Over the past few months, I have grown into my own skin and found my voice. Declan has helped me with this.

Keeping one elbow on the bar top, turning to face him slowly, chuckling, "We both make time and put in the effort. Something you could never do. Speaking of you, weren't you the one who was *fucking* someone else in our relationship. To answer your question, it's none of your fucking business."

"I had to get it from someone who was willing; seeing you were never home and always to God damn tired. Not to mention too big for me to even to want too," he said with a snarl.

Before I get a chance to respond, I feel Declan slide up to me grabbing my waist to pull me closer to him, "Let's get one thing clear, Jake. One, you will never speak to Evie like that ever again. Two, never speak about a woman's body image like that again or we will have a serious problem. And finally, thank you for fucking up royally as I have no problem stratifying her needs." Declan smirks at telling Jake in so many words he has no problem making me come. No, you do not sir. Declan puts a couple of bucks down on the bar and we leave.

After having the little run in with Jake, I had to help my sister fix her Bussell as it seemed to keep unbuttoning. I told her to get the French Bussell. Nope, she had to get the one button. I caught a glimpse of Declan speaking with my father and brother; they were laughing and drinking beers, so much better than when I was with Jake.

I would not catch them standing and talking with Jake as my family was never a fan of his. Feeling someone wrap their arms around my middle and spin me to their front; gasping and look to see it is my sexy date, my boyfriend. Declan whispers in my ear, "You okay about earlier, with Jake? I wanted to punch him so fucking bad from what I heard him say to you," he pauses taking a deep breath. His eyes get a shade darker blue laced with hunger before continuing, "I can finally touch you; I have been dying to all damn day. You in this dress and heels is making me think many dirty things I want to do to you. By the way, you are keeping the heels on tonight. You looked like a dream during the ceremony, babe." Declan tells me as we are slow dancing. I lean into him and kiss him softly.

"Thank you, babe. You in this tux is making me want to do dirty things to you, too. How sexy you look is this should be a crime. I could not keep my eyes off you either all night." I tell him as I wrap my arms around his neck, playing with the little hair he has on his neck, which gets me a soft moan from him.

"I like your dad and brother. They are good people and hella funny too. We were only simply shooting the shit, and they invited me back anytime. I think they may like me more than you. I mean, they wouldn't if they knew what I plan on doing to your body tonight," Declan says as he is playing with the skin I have shown in the back of my dress. With simply this brief touch has my panties soaked.

Little does he know what I have under this dress. A few days ago, Sophia and Grace came shopping with me to get some lingerie, and I have never worn this before. Deciding to step out of my comfort zone and surprise my man. I bought a new G-string thong, which is crotchless and a new lace matching bra. I wanted to get the garter belt to wear stockings, it would show under the dress I'm wearing. When he sees me stepping out of my dress to show him, he's going to lose his mind. I also bought a few things while shopping at the store, a few things we could try together. Only thinking about it has me hot and bothered, and I cannot wait anymore.

I stop dancing and he arches his brow at me and smile at him biting my bottom lip at him. I lean into him and whisper, "I cannot wait any longer and I think it is time to go to our room because you in this tux is making me so wet."

Right before we can sneak out, I am ambushed by Elise needing help again with her damn Bussell. This fucking thing is going to be the death of me. After settling the Bussell once more, I walk out of the bathroom to where I left Declan out by the side door. However, he is not here. Turning around again, I see him walking out of the men's room heading towards me. His hair is slightly out of place and his tie has been loosened. Declan grabs me by the waist pulling me closer, slamming his lips to mine kissing me with hunger. Breaking our heated kiss, he takes my hand to leave the reception, I turn my head as I heard someone stumbling out of the men's room and cursing, Jake. He is wiping his lip as it is busted wide open with blood trickling down staining his white dressed shirt. Not saying a word, turning to look at Declan who winks at me. Part of me should be upset on the fact Declan just beat the shit out of Jake at my sister's wedding, I even more turned on he was standing up for me.

I do not think we'd have left the reception any faster if we could after Declan beating Jakes's ass in the men's room. Could he be any sexier? Declan smiles and his right dimple pops out, and he winks at me while he takes my hand and drags me out of the barn. Giggling behind him as we make our way to his truck, all I can think about is him undressing me and seriously thinking about what it is making my clit pulse with need. I noticed where he parked was far away from the reception and I think he had an idea we would leave early.

Once we reach his truck, he grabs my waist and places me with my back against his truck, and his mouth crashes on my lips. This kiss is not like our normal slow kisses, no this is kiss is as if we cannot get enough of each other while my hands are in his hair pulling at it.

He growls into my mouth as I moan when his hand moves from my waist and finds the slit of my dress. I arch my back once he reaches my G string. He pulls back and we both are painting, "Baby, are you wearing a G string under this sinful dress?" He asks in his sexy raspy voice.

"Mmm" are the only words I can even put together at this point. I am so worked up; all I can think about is how much I want to fuck him against this truck right now.

He grabs my throat, not too hard simply enough to put some pressure. "Baby, you are mine and only mine. You in this dress is killing me, and I want you so badly. I do not think I can make it back to the hotel. I need you. Now."

Finally, finding other words to use, I say, "Please Declan, I need you too."

"Fuck baby! Okay, get in the back of the truck and this is going to be quick because all night you in this dress has been the biggest tease ever," his response with a deep growl.

He gets behind me while reaching for his truck's door,

"Remember the club and how I took you in the back hallway storage closet and fucked you hard?" He whispers in my ear while running his fingertips up my exposed thigh as I throw my head back against his chest as his fingers trace the outside of my G String. One inch and he will know how wet I am. He runs his tongue along my neck up to my ear.

I let out a soft moan. "God, yes. Please Declan. Please."

"Such a good girl. Climb in or your family will see me fucking you in this truck bed," he growls when he nips my neck.

We get into the back of the truck, and he unzips his dress pants and pulls them down, along with his boxers. Getting himself into position while I pull up my dress and he pulls down my G String, I go to stop him. He quirks his brow and before he can say anything; I straddle him, grabbing his thickness and guiding him to my entrance and sink down. We both moan in unison as he fills me. He grips my hips with force, and I move slowly while I grind up and down on him. He runs his tongue along my neck and slides his hand up to my throat. I absolutely did not believe it would arouse me with someone putting their hands around my throat, when he does it, I feel safe, and it makes me even wetter.

"Fuck baby! Your pussy feels so good. This pussy is

mine. Only mine." He stares into my eyes while thrusting into me.

"Oh, God! Declan! Yes… harder baby," I moan into his ear.

I swivel my hips in a way that drives him mad. Once I do, he grips my hips harder, and I know tomorrow there will be a bruise and I couldn't care less. I love when he marks my body. He thrust harder into me, and we are both so close as I can feel my release building and building. He removes a hand from my hip and brings it to the front of us and rubs my clit in a circle and putting some pressure…… I cum hard and my voice is something I do not even recognize.

"D… De… Declan I am going to…... Yes, right there, baby. Fuck!" I do not even recognize my voice.

"Fuck… E… E… Evie. Baby… I'm going… Fuck," he is growling. I feel his dick pulsate and I feel him cum hard into me.

We sit there for a few minutes gathering our breaths as we clawed at each other in the back seat. He lifts my chin up with this index finger and thumb so I can look at him, and then he places a soft kiss against my lips. "Okay, let's get you back to the room because, baby, I need to see what else you have under this sinful dress. You will cum on my tongue, my face, my hands and again on my dick. I am not done with you yet, baby. I want to take my damn time with you because I can't ever only have you once," he tells me as he nips my neck.

Smiling at him, I climb off him and adjust myself to the best I can in the back seat of his truck, and he does the same. Once we are decent, we get in the front seat of the truck. He reaches over and grabs my hand, brings it to his lips and places a gentle kiss on my knuckles, then he winks at me. How is this possible? We only just had mind blowing sex in his truck and I already want him again? I bit my lip, knowing I cannot have this man enough. The thought of this man makes me wet instantly.

nine

Over the last two months since Elise's wedding, my feelings for Declan are getting stronger, which should scare me at how fast I am falling for him, it feels right. At the wedding, he got along so well with my family, and they ask about him all the time. He and my brother already exchanged numbers with only a meeting once. They talk more to each other than I talk to my brother. I don't think Eddie even had Jake's number nor want to have it. I think Eddie only tolerated him for me. Seeing Declan getting along with my family and wanting to have a relationship with them made my feelings for him grow even more.

    I want to tell him how I am falling in love with him, I am not entirely sure how to say it and part of me thinks it is too early, I mean we have been dating for about four months and the first month was us meeting. I am not even sure he feels the same way about me, and I do not want to say *'I think I am falling for you'* to have him not feel the same way. If he does not feel the same, it would crush me more than walking in on Jake. The more I think back to my relationship with Jake, the more I should have seen the signs of leaving him. Being with Declan has made me see myself worth, that I matter, and I need to voice what I am feeling. Part of me thinks he might feel the same way I do; I simply need to tell him. I know I do because I am about ready to burst.

Shortly after Elise's wedding, Declan asked if I would like to come to a family dinner one night to meet his family. It seemed only fitting as he met mine and our relationship is moving in the right direction and becoming more serious. At least it feels that way. I am overly nervous to meet his family as Jake never brought me around enough to get to know him more. Declan is very close with his family as I am with mine, plus we both come from decent size families. I hope they like me, and I like them.

As I am getting dressed to meet Declan's family, my phone rings and Declan is calling me. Looking at the time, I still had another forty-five minutes until he was due to pick me up.

"Hey, baby," I say softly as I answer the phone.

He sighs, "Hi, babe."

I cannot shake this feeling as something is wrong, "Um, is everything okay? Are you going to be running late or do you need me to meet at your place instead?" Asking with concern in my voice.

"Evie, baby I am sorry, I just got called into the station for shift. Fucking bullshit! The lieutenant on shift, got injured badly on the call they were out on, he fell off the fucking roof. Fuck, it was a bad one too. He is fucking lucky though. I go in and fill in for his shift then I have mine too starting in the morning. I am so fucking sorry baby. I was so excited for you to meet my family tonight as I know they are going to love you," he tells me with a soft tone.

Holding back tears as I do not want him to hear me cry on the phone, "Oh, um okay. Maybe another time babe."

Declan sighs and curses, "No it is not okay, baby. I will make this up to you I promise."

Nodding thinking, he can see me, "Sure, baby. Have a good shift."

"Thank you, baby. I will call you when I have some downtime. Night, Evie," he tells me.

"Night," I respond softy.

I hang up the phone and the tears fall down my face. Thank goodness I had not done my makeup yet as my face would be even more of a mess. All those insecurities are bubbling up to the surface again as his work comes first. After all those years with Jake always putting our relationship on the back burner and never putting us first is coming right back at me. Looking at myself in the mirror, I see someone who is not worthy of love. I cry even harder.

"Are either one of you working tomorrow? I feel like we have been working so much and I need of a girl's night. Plus, Declan is working a double shift," I ask Sophia and Grace as we are sitting at the nurses' station dressed in our princess outfits. It was 'Princess and Frog' day on our floor. You're welcome nurses as I planned this one.

They speak in unison. "NO and YES!"

"Wait, are we second to your hot firefighter boyfriend? Because I mean DAMN…. GET IT GIRL." Sophia sign songs to me.

"NO! I was only stating he was working a double shift. Wait, you think I have been spending too much time with him and not you guys?" Asking with some hesitation.

"No girl, I am only giving you shit. You should spend all your time with the sex goddess." I get a wink from Sophia.

"I agree with Soph on this, but yeah, we miss you. You are still building this relationship with Declan. From what you told us about Jake, it was about him and not you. Declan looks at you like no one in the room who matters. It's hot," Grace gushes.

Blushing, "No he does not."

Grace and Sophia say in unison, "Yes, he does!"

I mean, it could mean what I think it means, right? The girls and I had a blast during our girl's night, and I will say it was much needed. Plus, the free entertainment of watching Sophia flirting her way through the bar was priceless. I swear this girl has no shame and it is amazing to watch. If I had a tiny piece of her confidence, I would be golden. Sitting on my couch relaxing re-watching Gilmore Girls because why not? The show is funny, and I am team Logan. I used to be team Jess, but Logan came out of nowhere and does care for Rory. Right when Logan and Rory are understanding what they are feeling for one another, my phone ringing, and I did not notice the number and I pounder if I should answer or not.

I picked up on the sixth ring. "Hello?"

"Is this Evie Cooperson?" The other person at the end of the phone asked with a deep raspy voice laced with panic.

"Yes. Who is this?" I asked in a stern voice because I have not have a clue who this person was. They sound panicked.

"Oh, I am sorry. Uh, my name is Tyler and I work with Declan. He, um, there was an accident during our shift while out on a fire call. They took him to Mass General about twenty minutes ago," Tyler tells me.

I cut him off before he finished the rest of his sentence. "What-what do you mean there was an accident?! Is he okay? Oh, my god!" I am trying to hold back the tears building up to as I am trying to hold back from releasing.

"Uh. Fuck. They rushed him in and we have not

gotten an update. I know he would want me to call you to let you know." Tyler sounds nervous, which is making me nervous.

"I -I'm on my way. I need to make sure he is okay." I am rushing around my apartment while I tell Tyler I am leaving.

"Do not rush and get yourself hurt; he would have my balls if he knew you got hurt on your way to see him. Oh shit, the doctor is coming. I will update you when you get here," Tyler lets out a breath before hanging up.

"Tyler… It's going to be okay. He has to be okay." I tell Tyler, letting out a deep breath. I am trying to keep myself together because I do not know what happened or how bad it is.

"He has to be Evie. For his family, his brothers… and you. I will meet you outside. Bye," He hangs up.

Thank God to the taxi driver he understood when I said, 'step on it'. Also, Sundays in Boston in the fall almost winter season is not too busy either. Paying the taxi driver and rushing inside like a crazy woman, I mean I am because the guy I am falling for had an accident at work and not knowing what state he is in. I notice a firefighter with blonde curly short hair, tall, maybe taller than Declan standing out front with his arms crossed, leaning against the wall, glancing up at the sky. Okay, are all the firefighters at Declan's station required to be built like someone from Sparta? Also, how has Sophia never mentioned him to me? She would be climbing him like a god damn tree.

I believe I recognize him. "Tyler?" I ask him quietly.

"Evie? Hey. You got here fast," he gives me a tight smile.

"Uh, yeah. So, what happened? And what did the doctor say?" I ask Tyler timidly. You would think being a nurse I would be calmer, or I'd think logically about the situation. Not when it is the person you love. Love? Do I Love him? Not now, Evie! Focus!

Tyler lets out a deep breath before telling me, "There was a structure fire down in Hyde Park. Our station does not usually service that area, as you know, the flames were coming out of every direction where a bunch of stations were called to help as it was starting to get out of hand. He is our lieutenant, so he makes the calls for our truck after the chief yells the orders. We were inside trying to get everyone out and only just gotten the last person out and Declan thought he saw someone or something in the back of the building. Over the radio, our chief told us to evacuate as the building was going to cave in the matter of a minute, Declan, being himself, told me to head out and he would be right behind me. I turn to follow him toward the back of the building," Tyler's voice gets a little shaky while takes a deep breath before continuing to tell me the rest of the accident.

"We were not even five feet from the area he wanted to

check, and the ceiling gave out came crashing down on both of us. He got the brunt of it; we were both knocked out from the collapse. After I got my surroundings and hearing our radios going off since we were immobile for a period.... I dragged him out of there. The doctor said he was lucky as the hit could have been a lot worse. He suffered a serve concussion and a dislocated shoulder and a sprain wrist. I swear to God this man has nine fucking lives, I tell ya." He is pulling the back of his neck while letting out a deep breath while telling me what happened.

Trying to take this all in and process what was just told to me, and what could have happened, I keep thinking, is this what it will always be like? I know me being a nurse is demanding and stressful, at least I leave not injuring myself or possibly die. I must look at Tyler like a crazed woman who is staring at him and not answering him.

"I know it is a lot to take in and to date someone who is in this line of work. This is more than a job for most guys here. It is a brotherhood like no other. When one of us gets injured, we all get injured. Everyone's spouses and significant others become family. You're one of us now. Before you see him, take a minute and go in clear-headed. It will crush him seeing you fearful," he smiles at me and next thing I know, he gives me a hug. I sniffle.

"Thanks, Tyler. He is incredibly lucky to have you and this whole engine behind him. Okay, I am ready to see him. Can you take me?" I smile and follow him inside.

Standing outside of Declan's room, I take a minute and gather myself because, like Tyler said, I do not want to show him how his job makes me fearful or even if I can handle this type of life with him. I turn the handle and let myself in, and as soon as he hears the door, he groans a little. "Ty, I told you I am fine and stop bugging me, Jesus. Bro, for real, it was not even that bad of a call, only a scratch." He lets out a jagged breath.

"Hi," I say quietly, hugging myself in the doorway with the door shut behind me.

He turns his head to the side and his eyes bug out of his head, "Evie, baby, what are you doing here? H-How did you find out?" he asks softly as it hurts him to talk.

Slowly walking over to the side of the bed, I grab his hand in mine, "Tyler called me. I rushed right over here to see you and make sure you were okay. Gave us all quite the scare, I will say." I tried my best to not cry, just seeing at him in this room with the wires and monitors, it could have been worse. The tears cover my face.

"Evie, baby, don't cry. I am okay and I am alive. Please do not cry, baby. I am so sorry," he whispers to me.

"Declan, I was worried. So scared, baby," I whisper to him as he takes my hand and kisses my knuckles.

He lifts the blanket and pats the bed. I kick off my shoes and climb into the small hospital bed with him. He puts the arm, with no wires or monitors, around me while I lay my head on his chest and listen to his heart beating.

He kisses the top of my head and we lay there together listening to the beeping. I keep thinking if this is the life I want to live; I know this could happen at any moment again, and he could seriously get hurt worse than today or even die on the job. Can I live with this notion? Can I be with someone again who puts his work first? I am not entirely sure I can, and it breaks my heart. I might have to let him go. The nurses were trying to check on his vitals as I lay in bed with him. I sit up and try to untangle myself from Declan. He is out cold thanks to the medicine they have been giving him, so I know he will not feel me moving to get up. I smile up at the nurse and mouth *sorry*; she is an older lady and winks at me. I look at my phone and it is way past visiting hours, and I need to be at work in four hours. I lean over the bed and give him a kiss on the cheek, and I whisper to him *'I love you'* because I know he will not hear me or remember it. Silently, I put my shoes on and leave the room. I am holding in a sob in the back of my throat as I will not let myself break down in this hospital hallway. No, this breakdown is going to be saved for when I am home alone in my shower, like any adult woman in this world, because my heart knows this is the end for Declan and me. I simply hope he understands. I am not even sure I fully understand.

ten

It has been two weeks since Declan's accident while he was on shift, and I will admit I have been dodging him a bit - Okay a lot. When he was first discharged from the hospital, I helped him back home and get settled, which was pretty much it. I have texted him here and there with the excuse we are short-staffed, so I have been working more. It is not a lie per se on working more, it's easier for me to dodge *'the talk'* with him. So, I figure if I simply work myself to the bone, then maybe I won't have to.

Sounds fine in my head, we all know this is only going to boil over…. I am seriously trying to avoid having everything erupt in my face. I know how crazy I am to leave this amazing man who makes me feel beautiful and treats me like a queen? After my relationship with Jake with him always putting his career before me is my own insecurities. I need to work that out. I guess, in hindsight, I should have done those things before jumping into this with Declan.

Finally, I have a day off after working what felt like months upon months. Sophia and Grace wanted to get together for dinner, as I am too tired to go out, let alone be functional. I take the hottest shower I can stand to wash the hospital off because when you work so many days back-to-back; you smell like one. It gets deep into your skin and the small sometimes lingers even after showering sometimes.

After my shower, I throw on my yoga pants, my UMAINE hoodie and put my hair into a messy bun. I do not plan on seeing anyone other than my door dash person. I ordered some takeout and then put on my Netflix and hit play on Gilmore Girls. When Rory is in college at Yale, she puts the Jess and Dean mess behind her. Watching my favorite episode, I hear a knock at my door…thinking it is my door dash when I open the door, when I look up; I see it's Declan. Damn it, he looks good in his dark blue jeans with his Engine Fourteen hoodie on with a beanie with the station's logo on the right side. I see he is no longer in a sling for his dislocated shoulder, which is great and means he might be back to working soon. I am assuming his doctor has cleared him because, knowing Declan, he was itching to get back to work. You might ask yourself why I don't I know this; well, I have been a shitty girlfriend and been kind, ignoring him by working.

I clear my throat, "Hey what are you doing here?" I ask him cautiously.

"Mind if I come in?" he asks dryly. Nodding and stepping aside, I let him. I shut the door behind me and move to the living room while he follows me.

He pulls me into him, which catches me off guard, and he kisses me gently. "I missed you. I have not seen you; we only have texted a few times," he says, staring at me directly in the eyes while he holds me. It feels as if he knows what is coming.

I clear my throat and pull away from him and go to move to the couch to sit. "Yeah, I have been working so much and we have been short-staffed lately." Pulling my legs under my chin, I gesture for him to sit.

He rolls his lips together and nods his head before he speaks to me, "You sure that is all there is? Work? Nothing else is going on? Nothing you want to tell me or?" I can feel the anger coming off him.

"Dec-" I do not even finish saying his name before he cuts me off.

"Evie, I ran into Sophia and Grace the other day and they said you guys are *not* short staffed as you have been picking up shifts like a madwoman. They are worried about you, then I put things together on when you started working so much. It was after the accident. Once you helped bring me home and got me settled, it was as if you could not get away faster if you tried. I tried to chalk it up to you were telling me the truth about how you were short staffed, and it was not because the accident scared you or call me crazy, second guess us," he says this to me with his voice stern.

I need to think about what I want to say so it does not send him over the edge, I need to be honest with him. I know I am going to fuck this up bad. "Umm…" I turn to look him the eye and say, "Yeah, I have been working a lot. Yes, Sophia and Grace are right. We are not short staffed." The last part comes out as a whisper. I am hoping he did not hear it, however I can tell he did by the way his body tenses up.

He looks down and shakes his head and then back up to me with his elbow on his knees, "Why, Evie? What is going on here? Did I do something? What is it?" He asks me in a shaky voice.

I take a minute and raise my head to look at him in the eyes, which was a mistake because I see hurt in them. And I know when I tell him on how I cannot be with him any longer..it will crush me more than him. I need to let him go when I am not even sure I can handle being put on the back burner again. Yeah, it's selfish. However, I have not healed fully from the breakup with Jake. Those emotions and feelings are still there, and they presented themselves when the accident happened.

"I… I… I can't do this anymore, Declan," it comes out as a whisper, and I think he does not hear me, then he whips his head around to look me right in the eyes.

"What do you mean you cannot do this anymore,

Evie? Please tell me what you are saying because it sounds to me *you* want to end what we have going on here," he says in a heated tone. I can tell he is trying to hold it together and, to be honest, so am I.

"Declan… being a firefighter is not only your job, but also *your* calling. It's your identity. You will always put being a firefighter first and everything else second. I cannot be with someone who, again, is putting their job before anything else. Yea, maybe I am being over dramatic here, this is how I feel right now. The accident you had a few weeks ago could have been so much worst Declan. So much worse," I close my eyes that are filling up with tears before saying, "You got lucky with a dislocated shoulder and a concussion. Answer me this? What happens when something even worse takes place while you are on the job, much worse and makes you give up being a firefighter? It would crush you." My voice raises the more I talk to him.

I pause before saying, taking a deep breath. "I honestly do not know if I can do this again, Declan. Maybe I have not dealt with my issues from my previous relationship, you will always choose to be a firefighter over me." I cannot stop the tears. They kept falling, and I let them. I need him to see he is not the only one affected by this. I am too.

He gets up and pacing and he turns around to look at me, throwing his hand in the air. "It's seriously like that then, huh? Going to throw away what we have been building? Jesus Fucking Christ, Evie, this is utter bullshit, and you know it. You're telling me *you want to end* this?" He is shaking his head at me and asks, "Do you even mean what you said to me when you came to the hospital, Evie?" He walks over to me and pulls me to stand.

Holy shit, he heard me say it. He remembers me telling him I love him before I left him in the morning to go to work. I thought he was dead asleep and would not hear me. Hence why I said it like a coward. I turn my head away and only whisper, "I'm sorry." I am even more of a coward when I cannot even say sorry to his face. Jesus, I am a fucking bitch and do not deserve this man.

He shakes his head again, "You're sorry? *YOU'RE SORRY....* That is all you have to say?" He raises his voice at me before he says to me, "I am fucking in love with you," he yells at me with anger and hurt in his voice. I wince when he does. He takes a deep breath before he asks me, "Look at me. Look at me in the face and tell me you don't want me to go, and we can make this work. Evie, I am hanging on by a thread here.... Please," he is gazing at me with tears leaking from his beautiful blue eyes, begging me.

Sniffling, I say, "Declan, I am sorry, but I simply can't."

He is staring at me in disbelief before he turns and walks to the front door. Before he goes to leave, he turns and says, "I hope you figure out what you want, Evie, because I know what I want. If you ever needed a clue, it was you and only you." He opens the door and leaves, slamming the door hard.

Once he has left, I sink down on the couch and only cry uncontrollably because I love him with every single fiber of my being, I cannot even say the words to him because he is right. I am scared. In retrospect, I under no circumstances felt the way about Jake that I do with Declan. It hurt me because of the words Jake said to me, his actions. This with Declan is ripping me to shreds in what just took place. I hurt this man deeply by being a cold bitch and a coward. The words were right on the tip of my tongue. I wanted to scream at him. Yes, I love him too, in my mind, being pushed aside scares me to open to this beautiful man. Yes, I need to figure out my issues, and when I do, I hope maybe I can have this with him. If not, then it is not going to be. I hear a firm knock on the door and I think he came back, when I go to open my door in hopes, he might still be there, and this is only a dream, but it is my Door Dash delivery. Some part of me just wants to make this right because I throw the door open. A short guy in his forties takes a quick step back. I'm not positive I think he gasped. Yep, gasped.

He holds up a white bag and looks at the attached receipt, "Um. Evie? You order Door Dash?" He's got a beer belly and is out in cutoffs and flip-flops. Still, his eyes stay trained on that receipt as though he is terrified to look my way. I must look like shit.

eleven

It has been the longest three weeks since I told Declan how I could not be with him anymore and, to be honest, it has been harder than I thought. Sometimes you need to let someone go if you truly love them, I was in love with him. Asking myself if I made the right choice or am I being dramatic? I have lost count on how many times I have hovered over calling or texting him. Thinking about my relationship with Jake and how long I put up with someone who put their work before our relationship and how it affected me. It carried over to my relationship with Declan. The entire purpose for moving to Boston was to work on myself and to find myself. I still do not even know who Evie is. And when I do figure it out, will I even like her?

Since my sister's wedding, I have taken much of my PTO, my brother and his family are coming to visit me today, so I should be excited to see them. The plan was for Declan to spend the day with us too so he could get to know them better and for him and my brother to fall more in love with each other. I wonder if they have still talked since our breakup. It would surprise me if they don't, if they still do it's because Declan is not someone to cut them off because they broke up with their sister, right? At least I do not think so.

I arrived at North Station right on time as their train is arriving from Portland, Maine. Not even paying attention as I am scrolling on my phone and telling myself not to text him. God, I want to tell him how sorry I am and to see how he is recovering. Lost in my thoughts, and I catch movement out of the corner of my eye and Nolan is running full force towards me.

I notice in time for him to jump on me yelling, "AUNTIE EVIE!!! I MISSED YOU!" I smile and try to gather myself as I almost wiped out in the middle of North Station.

"Missed you too, buddy. Jesus you're heavy! What the heck are they feeding you? Good God!" I laugh at him, trying to untangle him from my body.

Next thing I know is Rose running up too yelling, "AUNTIE EVIE! AUNTIE EVIE!" This time I was ready for the invasion. I spin her around, which makes her laugh, "Missed you too, my favorite girl," I kiss her head.

My brother- and sister-in-law walk up next, and we say our hellos and at least they do not jump on me. Thank goodness, because then I would wipe out in North Station, especially if my brother jumped on me, as he is two hundred and eighty pounds.

"Auntie, where is my main man Declan?" Nolan asks as he is surveying around, as if he thinks he is going to jump out and scare him. I was hoping no one would notice Declan's lack of appearance, only Nolan would ask me where he was. Sure, kid, keep turning the knife. I cannot blame them, as I have not said a word to anyone in my family yet about how we have broken up. Let's say I avoid the topic at all costs when we speak.

Before I can even say a word, my brother says, "Umm, I think Declan had to work and won't be able to join us today. I will tell him how you missed him today and I am sure it bum him out, too."

I am staring at my brother at a loss for words because either he is lying to help me out or he has been talking to Declan. McKayla leans over to me and whispers to which I can only hear and says, "If you are wondering if they still talk, yes, they do. He told Eddie he had to work today; however, I am sensing there is more to the story. Am I right?"

She looks at me and I only simply nod, and I am fighting back tears. Instead of drawing attention to us she grabs my hand and gives a tight squeeze letting me know she is here.

My brother claps his hands together and says, "Let's go, ya filthy animals, we do not have all day!"

We all played tourist today, and it was a delightful distraction from my broken heart. We are ending the day at Boston Common and letting the kids run around. Sitting down after walking around the entire city all day is when my brother decides this is the perfect time to ask me where Declan is. "So, I did not want to ask in front of the kids since they are fond of Dec, I take it he is not working today."

I let out a big sigh and holding back the tears, I clear my throat and keep my eyes straight. "Uh, I mean he could be, I am not sure since we broke up three weeks ago." McKayla reaches over to grab my hand.

Eddie shifts towards me more. "What happened Evie? At the wedding, it seemed it was moving in the right direction, and he was crazy about you. I mean hell, every single time at the wedding when someone mentioned your name, his whole fucking perfect face would light up."

He takes a minute before he says, "At Elise's wedding, Jake cornered him in the men's room before you and Declan left the wedding. Jake was running his mouth about you on how you are too much work, lazy, not motivated and your body is not attractive. Declan punched Jake so hard, that his lip split open spilling blood all over his shirt. It was impressive how Declan got none on him. Again, douche canoe's words, so do not punch me. Declan told him to fuck off and to never say a word or mention your name when he is around. And how Jake was not man enough to appreciate the woman in of front him. And he is so thankful for how badly he fucked up so you could find a real man who worships the ground you walk on. Again, those are Declan's words…" He chuckles, "I mean, I guess you're okay."

Then I punch him in the arm. "Jesus Evie, I said no hitting! Ouch, that hurt," he whines like a big baby rubbing his arm.

"What I am trying to say is Declan loves you and I think he knew it the night at the wedding. His eyes followed you all around that room when you were not next to him. So, what happened Evie?" Eddie asks me.

What Jake said to Declan hurts, just hearing what Declan said to him makes it hurt less. Woah, Jake was a piece of shit, and I was too blind to see any off it. Fuck him.

I turned toward my brother. "Declan did not mention any of the conversation to me. I asked him what happened, he told me he did not want to repeat what the asshole said to him. I did see when Declan came out of the restroom, he was a little disheveled and I did see Jake stumble out wiping blood off his busted face," I tell my brother.

McKayla grabs my attention and says, "Evie, did you

let what happened with Jake affect your relationship with Declan?"

I whip my head toward her, "Get out of my head Kay…yes, I did. He got injured badly but was lucky considering how bad the fire was that day. However, it was scary for me because this job he is going to put first. Jake put his work before me, and I did not want to be in another relationship where I felt second or even third. Yes, I know they are two different situations, I let my insecurities get the best of me and I have been beating myself up over it and I keep wondering if I am overreacting." I pause, wiping my eyes as the tears fall. "I miss him so much."

She smiles and says, "Remember when Eddie and I broke up in college?" I nod my head because I was thirteen when they broke up. She continues, "Your brother was busy with playing football, his classes, and on top of that he was the president of his fraternity. Did not help to add to a committed relationship which required his attention too. I understood he was busy. One night it became too much for him as he exploded on me saying how he could not do this anymore. He had too much on his plate and could not give me the attention he thought I needed. Now, remind you I did not ask your brother for time. Hell, I was fine hanging in his room at the frat to do homework or stay over. However, in his mind, he needed to give me more attention. I turned my heel and walked out. I told myself, if he loved me like he said, we would end up back together. It took some time and when I mean sometime, it was our senior year. After a year of waiting for your brother to get his shit together, I said 'screw it, I won't be young forever and it is a senior year of college'. I was at a party, and he showed up there."

She smiles as she tells me about the rest of the story. Before she continues, she looks up at my brother, whose jaw is tight. You can tell he does not like this part. "I was having a good time with my girlfriends. I met a cute guy and spent the rest of the party with him. Now, your brother had many other cleat chasers trying to get his attention, no luck. When the guy I was with at the party lean into kiss me, your brother marched his ass over and dragged the guy outside. Let's say there were words had and here we are all these years later. The moral to my story is sometimes it takes our minds a little to catch up with what our heart is feeling. If you love Declan and if he loves you, then you just have to let it happen." She smiles at me as the tears keep falling down my face. My brother's voice breaks my moment with McKayla.

"The guy had his hands all over you all night. He was an asshole," he growls at his wife.

"Yes, babe, but who did I leave with and who am I with now?" McKayla sang songs.

"Let's face it babe, you could not resist this," he wiggles his brows and I have all I could be to not punch him again.

I hug them both and tell them thank you because they

both gave me a lot to think about. We get the kids' attention and walk back to the train station for them to go home. I am sad to see them leave, after talking with my brother- and sister-in-law and I am feeling better. Maybe there is hope for Declan and me to patch this up.

twelve

After my brother and his family came to visit me a few weeks ago, I have only thrown myself more into working. Yes, after talking with McKayla and realizing my true feelings for Declan, I have yet to go to talk to him. Every single time I think about expressing my feelings to him, all I can see is the hurt look on his face the last time we spoke. What if this was all one-sided and if he did care, he would have fought more rather than leave. Right? Maybe I should take it as a sign as I need to let this go, try to move on with my life, what if this relationship was to be more than a few months? Did I seriously let this beautiful, kind, caring, thoughtful, fearless man walk out of my life without telling him how I feel? Am I that numb since Jake to not be able to see the best thing in front of me?

Not sure why I schedule myself to work four twelve-hour shifts in a row, I somehow think it's going to distract me from thinking about Declan. According to Sophia, I need to get my head out of my tight big ass, as she so nicely said. More like demanded, that is what I do. Grace said Jake obviously did some serious damage to my self-esteem, and she gets why I acted the way I did. She would have too, but she also sees Sophia's point too.

I am charting at the nurse's station as I find doing it when I am in the patient's room can sometimes be too distracting and it's better for me to write it down on my notepad and do it at the station later. Plus, I can note faster and not feel pressured to leave the patient's room. As I am finishing my notes for the next shift change, I feel someone's eyes burning a hole in the back of my head, and I already know it is. "Get on with Soph. Say it, I know you are dying to tell me again for the hundredth time," Letting out an enormous sigh.

"Well, if you already know what I am going to say, then I do not need to say it then bitch, now do I? Since apparently, I need to tell you *again*…. He is not captain of douche. Declan is a good man. A sexy man. You can't keep comparing him to a pencil dick, sweetie," Sophia is saying with her arms crossed next to me.

I turn in my chair and look at her. "I know. It's …" I look up at the ceiling trying to think of how I want to explain this and not to cry about this either, lord knows I have done enough of that, "It's all in my mind and at the time all I could think about was Jake putting his needs and dreams before mine. It was always him and I put up with it for so long. I was so used to it. And yes, I know Declan will have to put his job before me. I mean, we are in the same field. However, at the moment, it was all I could see. So, I thought if I took myself out of the situation, I would not get hurt… again. Unfortunately, I got hurt. It hurts so much more than leaving Jake or even catching him in bed with the captain save a hoe…. Soph seeing the hurt on his face broke my heart into tiny pieces." I can feel my eyes watering up and my face becoming wet as I am telling her this.

Sophia reaches for my hand and gives a good squeeze, "I know babe, it's because you are head over heels in love with this man. I am also known for a damn sure that he is in love with you too. You two simply need some time to get there. You will." I nod my head as it is all I could muster up to respond with.

One of the cool things about at working Tufts Children's was when the ER was short staffed or people were on leave, we could pick some extra shifts. I am sure you can guess. Yep, I picked up an extra shift a week because I am insane and I need to be medicated, or well, I need sleep and some tacos. We can work in either ER, the children's one or the regular ER. This time I opted to pick up a shift in the regular ER for a change of pace. I love working with kids, seeing sick kids day in and day out takes a huge toll on your emotions because no child should ever be sick. Look at my sweet Luca fighting cancer for a second time at the young age of twelve years old.

In the nursing world, we dream of taking an eight-hour shift rather than a twelve. It had been a tame night as the nurses I am working with informed me. Which was fine with me because a tame night usually means I might get to clock out early and I want to get some tacos on the way home, then hibernate myself for the next four days. Of course, when the thought appears into my head, there is a call coming in telling us there is a code blue coming in.

There was a car accident down by the North Station which the closest hospital is Mass General, however they are short-staffed, so we have been getting some of their overflow and this one of those instances. The head nurse on shift is on the phone telling us to prepare as it was a drunk driver who hit a person who was crossing the street. I swear it is never a dull moment here in Boston.

The person who the drunk driver hit apparently is a young male who now has serious injuries. Before we have a moment to catch our breath, the doors open and the paramedics are spewing off everything to Dr. Tray Marcelle, the trauma doctor who I am on shift with, as this is happening Dr Marcelle is listing off tests we need and what meds to push.

The patient codes, and I start doing chest compressions

while Dr Marcelle is getting the paddles ready. He yells "clear!" Thankfully we get the young man back into sinus rhythm. In the ER everything moves so quickly at lighting speed and especially at this moment.

After getting the young man stable enough we could transport him to surgery. If he pulls through, he has a long road of recovery ahead of him. As I am walking back to the nurse's station, Dr. Marcelle stops me by putting his hand on shoulder, "Evie, that was some fast reaction back there. Have to say I am impressed." He smiles as he says this to me.

Not going to lie, Dr. Tray Marcelle is one gorgeous man. He is tall, muscular but not overly muscular with the clean edge look rather than Declan's 'I'm all man who gets my hands dirty' kind of look.

I smile back at him. "Thank you, simply doing my job I guess."

Right when Dr. Marcelle goes to open his mouth is when I notice out of the corner of my eye a firefighter talking to the officers who came in to see the status of the young man who had gotten hit by the drunk driver. That was not what has piqued my attention. It's who the officer is talking too, Declan. I did not even notice he was part of the rescue scene who brought in the patient. The drunk driver only had a few cuts on him, which makes my blood boil.

He is even more gorgeous while he is working and

risking his life to save others. Jesus, did I royally fuck this up? The answer is yes. I make myself turn away and get busy charting on what had happened with our patient when I feel someone walk up to the nurse's station. As he was standing in front of the nurses' station, I was hit with his scent of sage and spice. All I wanted to do was throw my arms around him to tell him how much I missed him and loved him.

"Evie?" His deep rich voice makes my whole-body shutter. *Calm your tits, Evie. It is only his butterfly voice. You are the one that made the choice to walk away because of your own insecurities.*

"Hey," is all I could muster to say to this man who has been haunting all my thoughts for the last three months.

We both are starring at each other and were not sure on what to say. Declan is about to say something when the officer calls him over to ask him more questions about the scene. He smiles at me, not the one that would reach his eyes and make the dimple on his right cheek pop, more like a force smile. I know it is because of me.

The shift I picked up in the ER was an overnight shift and I was out at dawn. I looked down at my apple watch to see if Declan's shift is almost over too. After seeing him during my shift, I know I need to pull on my big girl panties and go over to his place to tell him how I feel before it eats me alive. I have enough time to go home and shower before heading to his place.

As I am walking up his steps to his house, my nerves are bouncing all over me. Feels like my whole body is shaking from being so anxious and I cannot remember the last time I felt this anxious in my life. I wipe my sweaty palms on my thighs of my jeans and then I knock on his door. I only hope he was not getting ready to take a nap as I remember sometimes, he likes to take a nap after a long stressful shift and, based on last night's shift, I would say so.

I hear him padding to the door and when he opens it, I can feel my heart in my chest drop. He has on dark jeans which showcase his tree truck thighs with a black Henley shirt which has a slight V-neck where you can see part of his tattoos, the tattoos I would love to run my fingers over. His hair looks like he simply rolled out of bed, and he has let his facial hair grow out with scruff. God, I have to squeeze my thighs together as I can picture his scruff rubbing against my thighs. This is man is too beautiful, it should be illegal. His eyes are wide as he was not expecting me to show up, well neither did I, buddy.

"Hi, Declan. Sorry if this is a bad time, I wanted to know if maybe you had a minute to talk?" I tried to get my voice to not sound so shaky, but fuck it, I am nervous as shit right now.

He leans up against the door frame, crossing his arms against his chest with his bulging biceps stretching in his Henley. He nods and gestures for me to come inside. I walk past him, and I smell his cologne and I seriously only want to melt into his touch like all the other times I have done.

I hear him shut the door behind me and him say, "What did you want to talk about, Evie?"

I am fidgeting with my hands, trying to the right words to say to this man, my Declan. *He is not yours anymore, Evie. You let him go, remember?*

I take a deep breath and look up. "Umm… I wanted to talk about us." I wince as I tell say *'Us'*

He presses his lips to a thin line and looks up still crossing his arms, when I move my eyes from the ceiling to look at him, he is already glaring at me, "You wanted to come over and talk about 'us' when it has been three months, Evie?" I can feel the hurt and coldness in his voice.

Nodding my head in response to him, "Yeah… Look, I am sorry it has taken me so long to talk to you…. I'm," I hesitate and sigh. "I'm not good at expressing my feelings to people or to people I care deeply about." The words are on the tip of my tongue as we are standing in his entryway. We have not moved since he invited me in.

He is silent for what feels an entity. "Evie, you are the one who said that you couldn't do this. There was no discussion after you made your mind up. I did not get a say in this at all. I told you how I am in love with you and it was as if you did not even give a damn about my feelings. Fuck, I still do, which makes me look like the dumbass here when you cannot even make up your goddamn mind on to what you want, Evie."

I can feel the tears rolling down my face as he tells me this, "Declan..." The words are right there, and I cannot say them. Jesus, what the fuck is wrong with me? Why can't I tell this beautiful man I love him too?

Declan bites his lip and simply shakes his head and chuckles. "I am one fucking sad piece of shit who is head over heels in love with you, you cannot even tell me how you feel, can you, Evie?"

"Declan... I..." I cannot even get the words out to him. The tears are rolling down my face faster at this point.

We are now staring at each other; Declan breathes heavily and moves closer to me and grabs me by the nape of my neck and slams his soft lips to mine. It feels like home kissing him. The kiss is hard, sloppy, and rough. Our teeth clatter and Declan is putting all his emotions into this kiss, and I am putting it right back. He pushes me against the wall, and I wrap my legs around him. I put my hands in his hair and tug at it, which makes him growl into my mouth and I moan a little.

He moves his lips to my jaw and then down my neck, whispering, "I've missed you, Evie. Please tell me you feel the same way. Please." I pull away from him and I look him in the eyes.

"Evie?" he asks me in a soft whisper.

I go to open my mouth; he goes to pull away from me and I drop my legs back to the ground. He clears his throat, "I think you should leave, Evie; I cannot do this again and have you break my heart a second time."

"Dec…" It's all but a whisper as he walks over to the door to open it for me to leave.

I go to kiss him on his cheek, cupping his face with my other hand. What I did not expect was for him to pull away from me. I know right now I have hurt this man so deeply by being a coward and not telling him how I feel. That is why I came all the way over to his place, for some reason, the words are stuck in my throat. Yes, I know I love this man and I cannot even tell him. All I can do is blame myself, and I do not deserve this man at all.

thirteen

Usually when I am on shift, I spend a lot of time with Luca and with Luca's family. I have grown very close to his mother as she has become a second mother to me over the last few months. I have seen Luca's reaction to this round of chemo and how it is starting to affect his body. Ice Cream seems to be the only food item he can stomach or even keep it down. Whatever gets him to eat, no kid wants the feeding tube.

Walking into Luca's room, I take a deep breath as each time I can see the cancer is slowly taking over his body as he has lost so much weight over the last few weeks.

"So, I had to lie to Debbie the other day on to why there were so many containers of rocky road ice cream in the nurse freezer. I was able to keep her off your trail for a little," I laugh as I tell him.

Chuckling, "Gosh Debbie is such a noobe."

Throwing my hands up laughing, "I am not even going to ask."

Luca sits up a little more in his hospital bed and I go to

the side of his bed, "Guess who came to see me the other day when you were not here?"

Rising my eyebrows at him, "Um, Tom Brady?"

Luca's eyes get wide as saucers, "I freaking wish it was true. Do not do that to me Evie, gosh, Tom is the Goat, the man, my love," he pauses before he says, "Nope, it was my other man, well, D-man, or Declan as you call him."

My eyes go wide and at what Luca just told me. I mean why would Declan come on his day off or when he is not volunteering? Does he do this on a regular basis? Or is he doing this to hurt me? So many things are rushing through my head at Luca's confession.

"Uhm, Evie are you okay? You look a little pale at what I just told you. Did you not know he came here sometimes on his days off?" Luca asks me timidly.

Clearing my throat, "Umm, no Luca I did not know this at all. Thinking about it more, it does make sense as he mentioned when he came here awhile back, he loves making the kids day brighter." I smile lightly.

"Yeah, well D- man, that is what I call him as we are bro's now. We play video games and talk about life. Man, he is so awesome Evie. Did you know Declan was the top firefighter candidate of his graduating class in the academy? He is like a real-life superhero man," Luca's face is light up like a kid on Christmas.

Smiling back at him, "No, I did not know that. I am glad you too having been hanging out." I go to stand up to fish out the medicine I need to give Luca and to flush out his port too.

Luca grabs my hand to squeeze it before saying, "Evie, I know I may be only twelve here but please do not cry too much over me. I know this time I won't be able to beat the big C. The doctors thought this might work, this kind of chemo. Trust me, me too dude. After speaking with my family, we have come to understand it will most likely be what takes me. So, please do not cry over me, too much. Okay, Evie?"

Trying to hold back the tears, I wipe my face with the sleeve of my fleece jacket, "Well, Luca you are wise beyond your years. I cannot promise I won't cry too much as you mean so much to me. Let's think positive here, okay?"

"Okay, Evie. Now, give me the good shit," wiggling his eyebrows.

Chuckling, I flush his port and push his medicine through his IV to him. Leaving his room after our talk, all I can do is not cry for him and what he is going through and the information he told me about Declan visiting him. How did I not know this information? He never said a word, no one did. Breaks my heart even more as he is seriously the perfect man, and I broke whatever we had. I truly do not deserve to have anyone in my life to feel love. I think taking the traveling nursing job might be good for now.

I looked forward to coming into work because of the patients I have and my co-workers because I love what I do. However, as of late I have not been wanting to be at work. I cannot stop thinking about Declan and what an asshole I have been, mostly Luca has been getting sicker. This poor boy is only shy of turning thirteen years old and has beaten cancer twice, this time it seems as if he will lose this battle. My heart breaks because Luca will most likely pass away before his thirteenth birthday, and I am not ready to accept any of this for him.

Charting away at the nurse's station, I hear someone walk up to the desk. I look up to see Mrs. Rossi, Luca's mom. "Hi Mrs. Rossi, is everything all right with Luca? Does he need anything? Do you need anything?" Asking her cautiously.

She smiles at me. "Oh, no, sweetie. I only came to check on you about how you are doing and how you feel after learning what the doctor had to say about Luca. You and Luca have such a special bond."

"Uhh...to be honest Mrs. Rossi, not really. He won't be able to beat cancer this time. I am so angry for him and for you. I am seriously praying by some miracle he can beat this. He should be able to live a full life. It is so unfair." I did not even realize I was crying at this point until Mrs. Rossi appears around the desk to give me a warm hug I so desperately needed. With everything going on lately with Declan and then to add in Luca, I break down and let all the emotions out I have been keeping in.

"Oh, Evie sweetie. I know how you feel, just sometimes the big man upstairs has bigger aspirations for us, and we cannot fight that. As a family, we have accepted this. As a mother, I have to accept what I am being told and Luca has to. Yes, cancer is one son of a bitch, we will remember what a sweet boy he was and celebrate him every day." I pull away from her hug to look at Mrs. Rossi, and her eyes glisten with tears.

I give her a faint smile and she says, "I will let you get back to work." She gives me one last hug and heads back to Luca's room.

I wipe my face and take a minute before heading back to the desk to finish my charting. The travel job seems better and better… maybe it is what I need, but didn't I move down here to start over? So, does this time feel more of me running away?

After the talk with Mrs. Rossi a few days ago, Luca has moved to hospice care, which is not in the hospital. They opted to do hospice care in their home, so when he passes; he is at home and in his bed. Gosh, I am not sure I could handle doing that with any of my family members. I was hoping they would keep him here so we all could be there for Luca, I understand. And Mrs. Rossi promised she would let us know when he goes. Luca was a popular patient and adored by everyone.

It is close to my shift ending when my cellphone rings, and I see it is Mrs. Rossi. I grab Grace's arm as she is next to me at the nurse's station. I got to slide the call button to answer, "Hi, Mrs. Rossi. Is everything okay?" I am holding my breath

"Hi, Evie… Sweetie. Luca has passed. He is no longer in pain. I am so sorry to call you and tell you this, I know you wanted to know, sweetheart." She is sniffing into the phone, and you can tell she is trying her best to hold back her tears.

The tears fall down my face, and I look at Grace, who is crying as well. "Mrs. Rossi, I am so sorry. Oh, my gosh--" I am at a loss for words.

Her voice breaks, "Oh sweetie, he knows you cared for him deeply." She breathes heavily before she asks me, "The funeral services will be next week, and I wanted to know if you will say a few words at the service. I know Luca would have loved that."

I take a deep breath, "Of course, I will Mrs. Rossi. Please text me the details."

"Of course, sweetheart." The line goes dead. I am left staring at my phone seriously in disbelief of the fact Luca is now gone. Who will walk up to the nurse's station to bug me? Who will scare me while I am doing rounds? Who is going to tell me useless facts about baseball? I am going to miss this kid so much.

When I finally look up from my phone, I notice most of the nursing staff from our floor are eyeballing me to see what they said. The look on my face and they already know. I finish my shift in a daze.

Luca's services are today, and I am not sure I can do this. Takes one last look in the mirror before heading out the door to meet Luca's Oncology doctor, Taylor McCrory. All the nurses have serious lady boners for Taylor, not me.

Doctor Taylor, Grace, Sophia, and I are all walking into the church for Luca's services. My body shivers, and I look over my right shoulder and lock eyes with Declan. His stare is soft, and then it turns too hard when he sees how close Taylor is to me. If it was him with another female next to him, yes, I would give the same stare. However, I am the idiot who walked away from that beautiful man. He is no longer mine and I am no longer his. So, another man can be near me.

How in the world did Declan know about Luca's services? I do not think he kept in touch with the family. Or did he? I think back to my conversation with Luca on how he would visit him when he had a day off. Feels like we are the only ones in the room until Sophia breaks our connection. "I told him." She whispers in my ear. Shocked is putting it lightly, surprised is more like it. I don't even speak and move to take my seat near the front, as I am walking down to my seat, Mrs. Rossi meets me.

"I am so glad you made it, sweetheart." I am trying to hold on to the hug she gives me. She pulls back and puts her hands on my cheeks, "He will always be with you." She kisses my cheeks and I simply nod my head.

During the service, I am so nervous to speak because I am not great at public speaking and because Declan is here with this entire station. I need to do this for Luca and his family. What pulls me from my downward spiral is Sophia nudging me as the priest called my name.

Taking a deep breath at the head of the church, I look at Mrs. Rossi, Mr. Rossi and Luca's brothers and smile with a slight nod.

"Hi, my name is Evie and Luca was one of my patients at Tufts Children's Hospital. Luca's smile was contagious, even with his constant flirting, he would joke about how one day when he is *older* that he would take me on a date." I smile and think of Luca telling me this.

"When I moved here from Maine and started working at Tuffs, Luca was one of my first patients and he thought it would be a great time to play a prank on the new nurse." I chuckle and shake my head. "He thought it would be funny to hide in the closet in his room. Now, it was not the hiding in the closet that was scary for me, it was the fact he had a clown mask on. A little back story, if you can guess I am terrified of clowns. I was searching around the room and even called the nurses' station to see if maybe he was walking around. Now, Luca was the biggest prankster on our floor, and I thought for sure thought that he wouldn't prank me. I found out later he pranks everyone.... When I go back into this room, he jumps out of the closet with the clown mask on. I scream and fall to the floor. He was laughing so hard, and I thought I was having a heart attack," I smile at the memory.

The whole parish is laughing, and I am smiling. I am peeking down at my speech. When I go to look up, I lock eyes again with Declan. I continue, "That boy knew how to light up my day, as well as everyone one on the floor. His goal was to make me smile daily as well as all the nurses, doctors, other patients and volunteers, and friends. Everyone who met Luca fell in love with him. I know I did. He would make your darkest days seem brighter even when he was in his darkest of days."

I feel the tears fall down my face. "I going to miss his smile, laughter, his countless random baseball facts, countless TikTok dances he would make me do with him and the flirting and his fearlessness. No matter how sick he was, you certainly did not know. He did not want cancer to define him, he would tell me -Evie, cancer can kiss my butt and I hope it smells too-. And I would have to say I agree. Also, he would want us to not be crying. He would want us to celebrate the life he lived and what he brought to each of our lives. He would not want us to cry if the Red Sox did not make it to the playoffs." I turn to look at his picture by the coffin and say, "I will miss you, buddy." I go to step down and Mrs. Rossi grabs my hand, and she squeezes it.

The services have ended, and we are walking out of the church. I feel his presence before I see him. Sophia asks me, "Are you going to take the travel job? I know you have been thinking about it."

Of all days and times, she picks now the time to ask me this. I know why she is doing it because Declan is in earshot.

I look over her shoulder where Declan is and say, "Um, yeah, I think so. I am meeting with the contracting service tomorrow." As I tell Grace and Sophia, I turn to see Declan's lips go into a thin line. I mean, what else does he expect me to do? I am being a coward.

She smiles, "I do not want you to leave, and I am sure Grace does not either. And I am also sure there is someone else who won't want you to go, either."

Still, mine and Declan's eyes lock on each other. I say, "Me too."

Sophia looks over her shoulder and back at me. "You sure this is the right move? You two are the most stubborn people I know. Have you tried telling him again? Him showing up today should mean something, girl."

Biting my lip and shaking my head, I say, "I do not even know what the right thing is to do anymore. I moved here to start over, and no; I have not tried talking to him again. He is showing his respects to Luca's family. Luca meant a lot to him, too. He is not here for me; I am happy he is here to support Luca and his family."

"Are you sure about that, girl? He has not stopped staring at you since you got here. And I'm also pretty sure he wanted to deck Doctor-Tight-Ass Taylor for even near you." Wiggling her eyebrows.

"Did you drink before coming here? You are reading into things Soph?" I ask her with concern in my voice. I mean, you never know with her.

"No, I have not. But I should have. Your speech made me cry like a baby. And I only speak the truth." She crosses her heart. What are we five?

I go to open my mouth and Taylor walks up and I look up to where Declan is. Maybe Sophia is right and maybe she is not. "Ready to go Evie and Sophia? I have to get back to start the shift."

"Right behind you, Doctor-Tight-Ass." Sophia winks at him as we walk to his SUV. As I am walking, I can feel Declan's eyes on me, and I am not sure I can handle the look on his face if I turn around.

fourteen

Hard to believe after moving to Boston merely over six months ago and falling in love with the city, my job, my patients, my new friends and, of course, Declan, I took the traveling nursing job for the next year. Yes, I am running from my feelings, and there is no turning back as I have already decided to leave. I leave for my first contract in five days, and I still have so much to pack and bring back to Maine. My brother- and brother-in-law are driving down tomorrow to load the truck up to bring some of my items to put into my parents' basement for me.

When I took over this sublet, I did not need to bring any of the furniture with me, as when I moved here, I did not want a thing from when I lived out with Jake. The items I do not need to take with me are only miscellaneous things like fake plants, pictures and sentimental items. This new traveling nurse gig has me no longer than a month at a place, so no need to re-pack everything every single time I move from job to job. This job, although will pay off almost if not all my debt from school and Jake, I will miss Sophia and Grace so much, as well as Declan. I do not think he knows I am moving, and to be honest, I think it's for the best.

The next morning, right at seven in the morning, I wake to my brother Eddie and brother-in-law Luke pounding on my door yelling, "WAKEY WAKEY PRINCESS!"

I groan and get out of bed and fling the door open, appearing like a freaking hot mess. I am in my bootie shorts, one of Declan's shirts I sleep in every night with my hair in the hot mess bun, with my hair sticking up in every single direction.

"Well, don't you look like shit on this fine morning, little sis," Eddie says, too cheerful for my liking.

"Oh, um, Evie you could, you know…. put… on…. umm, some pants." Luke gestures and looks everywhere but me. I look down and merely raise my shoulders and start walking back to the room while they are grabbing boxes.

Eddie yells, "Yo, are you going to help or--?"

"Yeah, you behemoth, apparently these are not pants, according to sir-embarrassed-of-bootie-shorts over there says I need pants." I turn and give a tide smile and turn back into my room to put on some yoga pants, a hoodie and a sports bra. Next, they will point out I have no bra. Jesus, it is so comfy not to confine our titties into those contraptions.

Meeting them in the living room, I say harshly, "Better?" They both nod their approval.

"Great, let's get this done and get back to Mom and Dad's." I gesture to the rest of the boxes sitting on my living room floor. As I go to reach for a box, my brother thinks this is a great time to give me his big brother's speech.

"Hey, I am proud of you for taking this job. I only wonder what you're reasoning behind it as you only just moved down here about six months ago," he stands and pulls me into one of his big brother hugs. They seem to always help; no big brother hugs will heal my broken heart.

Taking in a deep breath and count to five, glancing up at the ceiling before I turn to Eddie, "I mean what is done, is done. Yes, I moved down here after ending a long-term relationship to help learn how to love myself again and to put myself first. Now, I am taking a new job again. This way I get to travel.... so why not?"

I won't admit to him to why I am moving, as my heart cannot stand running into Declan again. Boston is a big city, yes, but it is also small, and I know I will run into him a lot. Plus, his station volunteers a lot on the pediatric floor, so there is always a chance of seeing his beautiful face. There are also the times where I pick up shifts in the ED or at Maine General. The last run in when I was working in the emergency department was hard enough. The way he was staring at me broke my heart into a million pieces, and of course I won't tell him my issues I have. Great Evie…. However, my brother knows I am pulling some bull shit over him.

He chuckles and shakes his head, "You know Evie, you cannot bullshit a bull shitter. You are RUNNING from admitting your feelings. Want to know how I know? Because I did this too. Remember what McKayla told you? You are my little sis thru and thru. Have you TRIED to talk to him?"

"Jesus FUCKING CHRIST, Eddie, yes, I tried. BUT I COULD NOT TELL HIM BECAUSE I AM A PIECE OF SHIT!" I am yelling now, with tears coming down my cheeks. I am already emotional over moving because I love this city so much already and I hate goodbyes.

Eddie walks over to me and pulls me into a big bear hug. "Fuck, Evie. I have only ever wanted you to be happy, and you were happy with him. The way you two look at each other is once in a lifetime to find that. I understand how you are feeling, I do. Take a minute and figure out what you want to say. Because if you wait too long, you will lose your chance."

Eddie continues to talk while giving me the best big brother hug while I sob into his chest. "It is hard to admit you are in love with someone when you are still dealing with issues from a toxic relationship. Sometimes we need to have a rocky moment to make us realize we deserve to be happy. If being with him makes you happy, then let's go get that man of yours. If you choose not to be with him and you being happy is being across the US, then I will support that too."

"All right, enough lovey dove crap. I need food." Luke winks at me. Eddie and I chuckle and pull apart. My brother-in-law and my big brother are very important to me. I seriously need to focus on myself and put Declan behind me and move on. I was too much of a coward to express my genuine feelings that I had for him, I will have to live with that and be okay with it. He was no doubt my person and I walked away.

It's the night before I leave for my first contract at my traveling nursing job and I am so nervous because I will not only be two plus hours away from home, now a few thousand miles away in Seattle. I keep making excuses for not talking to Declan because talking with my brother was not much help either. I am still a jumble mess. After two bottles of wine, which was probably not the smartest idea since I have an early morning flight tomorrow, I decide to write Declan a letter explaining my reasons, my feelings and why I have been such a coward.

During my wine intoxicated mind, I thought this was the smartest idea. Clearly no more wine for me if these are my ideas. Writing is the chicken way of expressing my feelings. And it is the only way I think makes sense. I obviously cannot voice them when I am around him, so a letter is the best way. My thought is to leave this for him at the firehouse and if I am remembering correctly, he does not work on Thursdays. He will get the letter hopefully tomorrow and I will be on a flight to Seattle, so he won't be able to bang my door down demanding answers. He will not know where to find me. Well, at least I hope not. I would not put it past him to be all stalker like.... again, the wine is winning here.

I get to the station, and I, of course, look for his truck or bike to make sure he is not here. Luck must be on my side, because neither is here. I walk up to the bay doors and a few of his fire brothers are working on the rig. One of them notices me and walks over to me... shit, it's Tyler who is Declan's best friend. I guess luck is not on my side, you shady bitch. Maybe my ass should have written him a damn email... nope. It's the wines' fault. Never again with the wine. I need to learn it never ends well. Get it together Evie.

"Evie? What are you doing here?" Tyler asks me in a firm tone. I mean, I do deserve it, seeing how I ended it with Declan, and I am sure he knows what happened between us and what I said.

"Hey, Tyler. I was coming here to drop this off for

Declan. Can you make sure he gets it... please?" Handing him the letter I wrote merely hours ago.

He looks at the letter I had handed him and looks up at me. "Yeah, I can, but Evie, as his best friend, I should let you know when you ended things with him. It crushed him. It crushed him more than when his ex was cheating on him with this friend. Man, I thought you two were it for each other," he chuckles.

Holding back the tears, which, of course, are from the two bottles of wine, that lead me here. "Anyway, I am leaving for Seattle for my new job tomorrow morning and I wanted to at least explain."

His eyes bug out of his head, "What the hell? I'm sorry, did you say *that you* are leaving tomorrow for Seattle? Or am I hearing things?"

Taking a deep breath, I tell him, "Yeah, I took a traveling nursing job for the next year, now I will go wherever I am needed. I need to learn who I am and who I want to be."

"Shit Evie. Does Declan know? If he does, he has not mentioned it to me," shaking his head, gawking at me.

"Not to my knowledge. Ty, can you please make sure he gets this and reads it? I want to make sure he understands my feelings and why I'm leaving now," I ask Tyler in a soft voice, I do not even recognize.

He smiles lightly and nods, "Sure Evie. I will give to this him when I see him later. Just so you know, when he finds out that you are leaving or when you have left, he is going to lose his fucking mind."

With that, I leave the firehouse and head back to the hotel before I leave early tomorrow morning. I only hope that he reads what I had to say and maybe it will help him understand why I said I couldn't do this. Yes, I love that man with every single fiber of myself. Who knows, maybe he has already moved on. If so, I deserve that.

fifteen

The new hospital I am working at in Seattle is much larger than Tufts, and I have gotten along with some of my colleagues here, not like my friends back at Tuft's. I must remind myself this traveling nursing job is not a gig where you make lifelong friends, however this is about me finding myself with having the great opportunity to travel all over.

After giving the nurses for the next shift the run-down on what happened on my shift, I feel my pocket vibrate and thinking it is Soph, Grace, or one of my family members I decided to check it once I get back to my apartment. The apartment of the traveling nurse company got me close to the hospital, so close as it is in walking distance, which I love. It is also within walking distance of all the cute shops and restaurants, too.

On my walk home, I stop by my new favorite sandwich shop to grab a late dinner and some essentials as I know once I am back at my new apartment, I will not go to want to go out again. I started a new routine since moving to help ease my broken heart and it is right when I get in from work; I place my dinner on the counter, strip off my clothes and take a hot steamy shower, then throw on my yoga pants and one of Declan's shirts. Yes, I may have taken a few and makes me feel close to him even though how everything ended. Sitting down about ready to take a bite of my sandwich, I hear a loud frantic knock at my door.

Sitting frozen with my sandwich halfway to my mouth, I think it must be a mistake because no one knows where I live except for my loved ones back home. I go to take a bite and there it was again. Okay, maybe it is a neighbor who needs some help and I am a nurse, is what I am telling myself. I get up and look thru the peephole and it is defiantly not my neighbor.

It's Declan. I open the door and he speaks first, "Evie, what the in ever loving fuck is this?" he says firmly, holding up the letter I wrote him over a week ago breathing heavily.

I must remind myself to stay calm and not let him know seeing him is has a powerful effect on me. Lord knows that's a goddamn lie. I say smoothly, "A letter I wrote to you before I took a new job."

He presses his lips into a thin line, peering up at the ceiling before returning his glare back at me. The next thing I know is he is crashing his soft lips on to mine. Oh god how I have missed his lips, his touch, his smell, his everything. I melt right into him and place my arms around his neck, which he grabs a handful of my ass and hikes me up. I wrap my legs around him while he pushes us through my doorway, then slams the door shut with his foot.

He spins us around so my back is against my door and in between our frantic kissing he says, "You thought a letter would help ease my broken heart, Evie? You thought I would be okay with that?"

Staring in his blue eyes, I love so much; I can tell exactly how much I have hurt this man with my insecurities. How could I not have seen how much he loved me and how much this bothered him? I honestly thought he would simply move on. Isn't that what all men do? Not Declan, not this man. When he loves, he loves with his soul and loves me deeply. Him showing up here in Seattle is showing he cares, and he wants us. I at least hope that was why he was here.

"Declan, what are you doing here? Because Boston and Seattle are a tremendous feat if you are only wanting to know about the letter, I wrote you." I ask him, with my legs still wrapped around his middle, with his erection pressed against my belly.

He takes his hand, cups my face with his thumb caressing my left cheek. I melt into his hand, "Because Evie, this was the first time you were honest with your feelings with me. It sucked fucking balls that you had to write it in a letter, you finally told me. I have been waiting months for you to do that. It messed with me because I thought my feelings were one sided." He pauses and then smiles, "When I had a moment, I caught a flight out here and after some sweet talking to Eddie, I got your address. I had to come to you Evie... I wanted to make sure you still felt this way." I can see the question in his eyes and the hopefulness. Taking in this beautiful man who loves me with his whole soul, yes, I love this man.

"Yes," I reply in a soft whisper is all I can get out.

"Yes, to what? Yes, you feel the same. I need to hear you say it, baby. I need to hear it so badly," he pleads with me.

Gazing straight into his eyes, I smile. "Yes, my feelings for you have not changed. You are all I think about and all that I want. I love you Declan."

He smiles so big, and his right dimple pops out, "Thank fuck. I love you too, Evie, so goddamn much." He leans in and whispers against my lips, "Now I can fuck you against your door and your neighbors will hear or I make love to you all night. Which is it?"

Jesus, this man and his dirty mouth. I am soaked, shit I was soaked instantly when I saw him on the other side of my door. I lick my lips and say, "Make love to me."

His lips crash on to me again and he walks us back to my bedroom. This apartment is a one-bedroom, so he does not need for me to tell him where my room is. Once we get into my bedroom, he sets me down. He pulls away and sees I am wearing one of his shirts. He smirks.

I go to take it off, he goes to me. "No baby, I will be the one doing the undressing, as my hands are itching to touch you." Well, God damn.

He removes my shirt, and I am braless since I took a shower when I got home. He then removes my yoga pants and then my underwear. I am standing in front of him naked and I do not feel ashamed of my body, no I feel like the most sexist woman. That is what Declan does to me. He makes me feel like the most beautiful woman; he makes me feel sexy. I arch my brow at why I am the only one naked. He then gestures for me to undress him, and I do gladly. I remove his hoodie and his t-shirt, then I unbuckle his pants and let them fall to the floor. I drag down his briefs and I lick my lips as his beautiful cock springs free. How I have missed this man's beautiful thick cock. I have spent many nights picturing it while I got myself off. It was not the same. I go to stand up and I slowly take in what a lucky son of a bitch I am to have this Adonis of a man.

He walks toward me and says, "Baby, I have missed this body." It sends shivers right down my spine.

He slides his hand up the nape of my neck and kisses me softly and he slowly lowers us on to the bed without breaking our kiss. I spread my legs for him to fit between. He is kissing my jaw, my neck, my collarbone, my breast where he licks my nub. That makes me arch my back and gasps. He then sucks and nips my cup before moving to my other breast. Slowly he moves down, licking and kissing my belly, moving to each of my hips, following the same steps. When he is in front of my pussy, he smiles and raises his eyes to look at me.

"Baby, I am a starving man. I am dying to taste your sweet cunt, as it has been too long." He dives in and spreads my legs wider to smoother his face between my pussy. Jesus, this man truly has a gift with his tongue. After he licks my clit with a slow-motion, he flattens out his tongue and then adds two fingers. He is pumping me faster with his fingers. He growls into my sex and the vibration against my clit sends me about over the edge. I am moaning so loud that I do not care who hears me.

"Declan yes…. Fuck yes baby…. right there." I can feel my orgasm building and I am about to explode when he curves his fingers, hitting my g-spot and nips my clit. I cum so hard I am shaking.

"Declan!" I scream and I feel the vibrations of him chuckling. He does not stop, he keeps going and I am not sure I can cum that hard again, to which my body shakes uncontrollably. I am holding his head between my thighs and pulling his hair hard. He growls.

"Baby, shit. Yes, I am going to come again." Moaning loudly.

I can feel the pressure building in my stomach and my

clit is pulsing against his tongue. This second orgasm is coming on stronger and before I know it, feels like I am peeing on his face as I cum the hardest, I have ever done, screaming his name. I mean, did I really pee on him? Panting as I am trying to regain myself, Declan raises himself up and wipes his mouth with the back of his hand. "Jesus, woman, you soaked my face when you squirted. Baby, you're delicious. And I am not done with you yet. As I plan to make you soak my face again, baby."

He lines himself up with my entrance and slams into me with us both moaning together. He feels like home. I crash my lips to him, and I taste myself on his lips and it makes me even more wet. He thrusts into me. "Baby, harder please," I say, peering into his eyes.

"Evie, I want to take my time with you," he says so sweetly.

"Declan, please. I need you to go harder, baby," it's not a plead, more of me telling him.

Without missing a beat, pounding into me. I grab his ass and pulling him even closer to me. Growling, he hikes my leg around his left side and lifts my hips slightly, where he has more access to thrust into my deeper. "Hold on to the headboard, baby."

I grab on to the head bard and slamming into me so hard the bed is moving. I am chanting so loudly, "Fuck Declan! Oh my god, yes!"

He is growling, and it is the most sexist thing. He

moves his hand to the front, and he is circling my clit. The pressure is all I need for me to explode, "Declan!"

One more thrust and he screams, "Evie, baby! Fuck!" Before clasping on top of me with his head tucked between my neck and shoulder. I am still holding the headboard painting, trying to catch my breath.

He looks up at me and smiles. "I love you so much," he kisses me softly. I pull my arms down and wrap them around him. He kissed me and I smile into his kiss.

When we break apart, he gets up to clean himself in the bathroom. He walks back to the bed with a warm washcloth to clean me up, too. Throwing it onto the floor, gets into bed with me, pulls the covers up while pulling me into him. My head is resting on his chest with my hand on his stomach as he drapes his other arm around me. I am moving my hand up and down his abs while playing with his happy trail.

We are both silent for a few moments until he speaks. "Evie, I do not want to lose you again. Before I went to see you in person, I thought a lot about us. This new job is for a year and it means a lot to you. I guess what I am trying to say is, I do not want to end what we have. I love you too much, to which I cannot go through it again." The emotion in his plea is audible to me.

I move to shift to look him in the eyes, "Declan, me either. It broke me leaving you and I was such a coward and expressing and not explaining my emotions is not something I am good at. I know I need to work on it. I also need to work on my insecurities that are from my past relationship. I do know I want this with us. I love you more than anything." I feel the tears sliding down my face. He wipes this with his thumbs.

He pulls me in for a gentle kiss and wipes my tears away with his thumb, "Then we agree. We are doing this. One year is not too bad. We can facetime, fly back and forth. I love you too damn much Evie."

I smile, "Me too Declan. Me too."

He pulls me on top of him and I know without a doubt this is the man for me. I have met my soulmate when I least expected it. My mom was right when she said there will be a man who will love me for me and will accept me for me. I will not let him slip through my fingers ever again. I love this man with all that I have.

END.

epilogue

Declan, Five Years Later

Those three shifts of twenty-four hours take a toll on your body as you get older, and fuck, I am not a young asswipe anymore. Lately, it seems there have been more distress calls and fires in the city and I am not sure how I am feeling about that. Although, I will say it is one of the best jobs in the world. When I am about to get up and start the day, I feel my wife crawl into bed with me. Crazy what life has thrown at us in the past five years, and I am so grateful to have gotten her back.

That first year with Evie being a traveling nurse was hard as fuck. We got through it, and I will say I am thankful for FaceTime because, goddamn it, did that help us out, a lot. I will say it sexy as hell, too. Once her contract was up, Evie moved back to Boston. I should say moved in with me to my house in South Boston.

Not too soon after she moved in, I proposed to her because I did not want to wait another day without asking her. You can guess what happened six months later, too.

Yep, we got hitched. It was one of the happiest days of my life to watch the love of my life walk down to me as her father gave her away. It was a simple small ceremony with only family and a few close friends back in Maine.

Evie returned to Tufts when she moved back here, which made her happy to be back working with her two besties, Grace and Sophia. Through the wedding night, I wanted to knock up her right away and by sure luck; we got pregnant on the first try. The second-best day of my life is watching my beautiful wife give birth to our baby girl, Aurora Fitzgerald, and I could not stop smiling at how beautiful and perfect she is. I fell more in love with my wife that day as she gave me the best gift, my daughter and for making me a father.

I feel her hand running up my chest and she snuggles up close to me. I wrap my arm around to bring her closer. It is rare for us to get this time alone when we have been on back-to-back shifts, then factor in our four-year-old daughter. She gives me a soft kiss on the center of my chest and makes me smile and makes my morning wood even harder.

"Morning baby," I chuckle, and she slowly brings her hand down to the top of my boxers, and when she grabs my big aching cock, she runs her thumb over my crown. "Mmm baby, that feels good."

Evie pulls my boxers down and then gets on her knees and before taking my cock in her mouth, she looks up at me and gives me that sexy smirk. She licks the pre-cum I have at the tip, and she swirls her tongue around my crown before she takes it all in her mouth. She is sucking hard and swirling her tongue as she does it. Cupping my balls, giving them a hard squeeze, "Jesus fuck Evie… just like a baby…. Fuck!" this woman is deadly with her mouth.

"Evie…. Ba… B…. Baby…. Fuck yes…. god damn you look so sexy like that taking my enormous cock in your mouth." Moaning as I thrust into her mouth deeper. My girl knows how I like it and how to handle my thick cock. She moans as she takes me deeper and the vibrations sets me off.

"Evie," I whisper as I do not want to wake our daughter.

Evie takes all my come down her throat and lets me out of her mouth with a 'pop'. She climbs up and lays next to me. "Morning to you too, baby."

Rubbing my thumb across her bottom lip, "A good morning indeed, baby."

We are staring at each other until she breaks the silence. "I'm pregnant," she whispers to me.

Smiling like the chestier cat and crash my lips to hers. God, I cannot get enough of this woman's lips. I pull back and look at her, "I knew last time was the one baby. Aurora is going to be happy to be a big sister, and I am over the moon. How far along are you?"

"Your ego is too big for this house sometimes. And yes,

I know she will be one great big sister. I am eight weeks along. Is it wrong I am hoping for this one to be a boy? I want him to be like you. You have the biggest hearts know, and you are the best daddy to Aurora. Watching you with her makes me love you even more than I already do. How did I get so lucky to *slam into you* all those years ago in that pub?" The tears fall down her cheeks. I take my thumb to brush them off her beautiful face, and I kiss her soft lips.

"No baby, I am lucky one to have *slammed into you*. As you were meant to be in my life to make it better in so many ways. You are the most caring, sweet and stubborn woman I have ever met, next to our daughter. 'I wink'. I also fall in love with you each day as I watch you being the most attentive mother while working full time. And I will love this baby boy or girl. I love you, Evie Fitzgerald." I tell her, holding her face.

"I love you too, Declan Fitzgerald." She pauses, "Now, make love to me before our four-year-old is bursting in here, because of this pregnancy I am so horny all the damn time."

Flipping her over on her back and slamming right into her with us both, moaning in unison, "Anything for you, my wife of mine. Oh, I think I can help with that anytime you need it, baby. Because I can never get enough of you." I bend my head down and I kiss her.

"I love you, Declan," she whispers.

ACKNOWLEDGMENTS

Thank you for reading this book and going on this journey with me, telling Evie and Declan's story. This is my first book that I have ever written, and it is my baby that took me just about a year to write. I love reading romance and smut books, I had this story that crossed the lines of personal and fiction. This has been something I have wanted to do for some time, so thank you.

Now, I would like to thank my husband for putting up with me this past year on writing this book and encouraging me along the way. Even when I was at my wits end thinking that I could not do this, he was right there telling me "YOU CAN DO IT." He was so proud of me writing this, that he was telling everyone he knew that his wife was writing a book. Thank you, hubby!

My girlfriends and you know who each of you are. I want to thank you for the support you have given me over this past year as well. You all pushed me and encouraged me like the little freaks that you are from the sidelines. I looked at each of you and took pieces of your stories to add to this book. I feel that all the characters are a piece of you in here.

Thank you to my mother, who encourages me to keep pushing through on writing this book. Thanks Mom, and please do not judge on reading some of this.

Please follow me on my Instagram and TikTok for more on what is coming soon. Kisses!

ABOUT THE AUTHOR

Nicole Waterhouse is a mama to two littles, a wife, taco lover and caffeine addict.

Living in Southern Maine, Nicole loves spending all her free time with her family.

Being an romance reader enthusiast, with her favorite tropes being YA, Mafia, reverse harem, second chance love, age gap, and more.

Nicole loves when the heroine is curvy and plus size as those heroines need their light to shine as well.

instagram.com/author_nicolewaterhouse
tiktok.com/@author_nicolewaterhouse

Made in the USA
Middletown, DE
14 September 2022